ESCHATONUS

Ray Adams

Copyright © 2022 Ray Adams

All rights reserved

The characters and events portrayed in this book are fictitious. Any similarity to real persons, living or dead, is coincidental and not intended by the author.

No part of this book may be reproduced, or stored in a retrieval system, or transmitted in any form or by any means, electronic, mechanical, photocopying, recording, or otherwise, without express written permission of the publisher.

ISBN-13: 9798808410138

Other books by Ray Adams

THE FORCEK ASSIGNMENT
THE JOLLET PROCEDURE
THE LAST SANCTUARY

As James Kinsley

PLAYTIME'S OVER

linktr.ee/rayadamswriter

Thank you, Vuvu.

FOR ALEX

I

Dawn over Netaris. It was quiet, with the occasional snatch of birdsong floating over the gentle breeze. Every now and then the low hooting of an unseen, nearby primate sounded. Aecola, high in the canopy, felt very removed from the forest life she knew she would be able to hear were she at ground level; the snuffling, crackling, buzzing and calling that made up the soundtrack to daily life on the forest floor. Up here, there was little sign of activity. If she took the time to look at the branches of the tree the outpost was mounted in, there would be insect life in abundance, of course. But aside from the occasional butterfly, looking out from the platform up here, the forest seemed still, at peace. An ocean of green, gently undulating as far as the eye could see.

She was peering through a set of binocs, scanning the forest for signs of logging. "This is just so strange..."

"What's strange?" Bokka came out of the tree house carrying two steaming cups of tea, one of which she held out to Aecola.

Aecola lowered the binocs and took the tea from her. "I thought we had a hit. Low-bed flier came in from the direction of Talos and landed about three klicks over there," she said, pointing. "But that was two hours ago and there's been no activity since."

Bokka shrugged. "Survey team?"

Aecola took a sip from her cup before placing it on the platform's broad railing, then raised the binocs again. "Maybe. Odd though, this whole sector's been surveyed within an inch of its life, I can't even imagine what they'd be looking for now.

According to Russell, this site's a natural target for a logging camp. No mineral wealth to speak of and the hargar wood's high quality. There's literally nothing to stop them from setting up a camp here, but there's not been a flicker of movement since they landed."

"Scientific mission?"

Aecola shook her head. "The latest update to the universities' mission calendar came through last night, nothing scheduled in this direction for six months. Unless it's off the books..."

Bokka put her cup down next to Aecola's and held her hand out for the binocs, which Aecola duly passed to her. She followed where Aecola was pointing to try and pick out the site but, as Aecola said, there was nothing to see. "Two hours? You want to go take a look?"

Aecola was already tying back her long, black hair into a hasty plait. "Took the words right out of my mouth."

The hargar forests of Netaris had been a bone of political contention for some years now. In the six decades since Netaris had been accepted into the Federation, they had been the source of Netaran wealth, hargar wood being an unusually strong hardwood, highly prized in construction. For all that time, the timber industry had been responsibly monitored, with quotas and repopulation a priority, but three years ago there had been a sharp shift in the planetary elections. Control had passed over to the Netaran People's Party, a far-right populist party that, in effect, was little more than a front for the handful of corporations that sat at the top of Netaris' economic food chain. Regulations had been slashed. Where they still existed, companies were logging indiscriminately anyway. Local government power to police illegal logging sites was limited and an ecological disaster was brewing, both of species loss and land erosion.

Aecola and Bokka were part of a network of activists who had answered the call and taken it upon themselves to monitor and report as much of the illegal logging as they could. Mostly, the companies paid their fines, brushed off the bad publicity and carried on. Only occasionally were the activists successful in shutting an operation down. Meanwhile, an army of lawyers had been put together by the more responsible wealthy elites of Netaran society, who were also bankrolling the activists. They were taking the issue to the Galactic Federal courts and this was seen as the only realistic, long-term hope for the forests. A federal edict to restore the preservation regulations and effective federal enforcement were the only things standing between Netaris and ecological meltdown, but the wheels of galactic politics moved slowly. Until then, grassroots activist groups like the one Aecola and Bokka belonged to were doing their best on the ground. The feeling was, though, that the movement was fighting a losing battle.

It was a pleasant enough hike, although not an easy one. The undergrowth was thick in that part of the forest and, this far from any major settlements, there were few paths. There were pockets of indigenous settlements dotted around the forest but to all intents and purposes, this was true wilderness. Aecola and Bokka had been out here for three months, however, and were well used to the slog.

They carried light backpacks, with just enough food for a day's excursion and their recording equipment. Bokka also carried their satellite uplink, so in the event of anything serious they could send data out without having to go back to camp. They chatted as they walked, mostly about professors and other students back at the University of Talos, where they had been studying before taking a sabbatical to join the monitoring programme. The university had committed to supporting the programme, so their places were being held for them until their assignment was over.

Bokka was Netaran, born and raised in Talos, so for her the fight was deeply personal. Good humoured, tall and muscular, she was a key player on the university's Plomo-ball team. As a result, her time in the field was ending early in just a few weeks, in order that she could be back for the start of the season. That hadn't been her choice, but the university had stipulated it as a condition when she signed up for the monitoring programme. The university Plomo-ball League was financially significant to the establishments involved and they couldn't afford to lose one of their star players for the first two months of the upcoming season. Bokka wore her dyed blonde hair short, and her arms were heavily tattooed, a cultural marker of her Netaran heritage.

By contrast, Aecola was an off-worlder, an Ekkaran. She had come to Talos for their Environmental Sciences programme, considered the best in the quadrant, her passion for conservation almost a vocation. Back home on Ekkaris, they were entering a period of technological and industrial upheaval and Aecola was determined to be at the forefront of the movement in terms of ensuring that the development didn't come at the cost of a healthy biosphere. Like most Ekkarans, she was dark-skinned, dark-haired and slight, with vivid violet eyes. Less ebullient, more studious than Bokka, she and the Netaran had nevertheless been firm friends since Aecola had first arrived at the university, bonding quickly in a shared Foundational Maths course. They had signed up for the monitoring programme together. Aecola followed now behind her stronger companion, her breathing only slightly laboured as she worked to keep up.

They were getting near the approximate area where Aecola had seen the flier come down. They stopped talking and slowed down, spreading out but keeping each other in sight as they carefully made their way forward, slowly, as per their well-rehearsed approach protocols. The loggers didn't take kindly to intervention and so there were strict rules on how close the activists were supposed to get to the camps and how much attention they were allowed to draw to themselves. Mercifully, to date, there had been no fatalities, but some students had been roughly treated in the past.

Aecola's heart rate was rising, and she was focusing on her breathing. She had a pretty good fix on where they were headed, so wasn't too concerned about missing the landing party. The concern was whether the loggers, if that's what they were, had spread out or were heading towards them even now.

Bokka stopped in her tracks, crouching down noiselessly and gesturing at Aecola to do likewise. The two stayed where they were for a minute or two, before Aecola slowly and quietly made her way over to where her friend was poised, watching.

"I thought I heard something," whispered Bokka.

They waited another minute, but all they could hear was the

regular sounds of the forest... Wait, no, there it was. Voices. Coming from somewhere ahead. The two activists inched their way forward. The voices grew louder. Still indistinct, no words were intelligible, but there was no doubt about them now.

The two young women reached a point where the ground dipped sharply, opening out into a small clearing at the bottom of the incline. Concealing themselves behind a thicker stretch of bramble, Bokka carefully lowered some of the branches until the two could see down into the clearing.

There sat the flier Aecola had seen earlier, its low bed empty except for a pair of heavy-duty crates, about a metre in length. In front of it stood half a dozen men. Two of them appeared to be in conference, comparing readings from handheld devices and talking quickly. The conversation was animated, if not overtly emotional. Clearly, they were disagreeing about something but there was no visible animosity between them. The other four men seemed surprisingly indifferent to the discussion, completely ignoring it. They were all armed, holding their pulse rifles in readiness and keeping an eye out in all directions. None of the men, Aecola realised, were local indigenous people, who usually made up the logging labour forces.

"This is not good," whispered Bokka.

Aecola frowned but didn't respond. Bokka was right, this was really unusual. The armed men weren't in uniform but something about the way they held themselves suggested military to Aecola, properly trained military. This was no tinpot logging company survey mission, that was for sure.

A seventh man appeared from the flier's cabin. He strode over to the two men arguing and said something brief that seemed to cut the men off mid-flow.

"We need to get closer," whispered Aecola. "We need to hear what they're saying."

Bokka shook her head. "They're armed, Aec. That is not a good idea."

"Wait here then, I'll go, I'm smaller, lighter on my feet."

Bokka looked dubious but didn't try to stop Aecola as she started to ease herself out from behind the bramble and down the slope, taking great care to remain hidden. About halfway down she stopped, giving a nervous Bokka the thumbs up from her new vantage point. Aecola pulled out her datapad and started recording the scene in front of her.

"... problem is that the readings aren't conclusive."

"There's a seventy-five per cent chance the make-up of the local flora at this altitude will provide the necessary conditions for successful dispersal..."

"... and a twenty-five per cent chance that it won't. We need to be sure."

The newcomer held his hand up, silencing the two men.

"Final thoughts, gentlemen."

"We cannot guarantee successful infiltration at this site," said the shorter of the two, pushing the glasses back on his nose.

"Given the health of the eco-system, the proximity of the nearest town and local wind patterns, this site fulfils our remit more fully than any of the alternatives. Jens is right, there are no guarantees, but this is the most likely place," replied the other, a larger man with a thick beard.

"Your evaluation is noted and I acknowledge your warnings. You won't be held accountable if the mission doesn't succeed, don't worry. We know there are no guarantees. That said, ultimately, it's my call, so I say we're a go."

The two men pocketed their devices and nodded, neither of them adding anything further.

Well, no doubt who's in charge, thought Aecola. The decisive man was above average height, well-built and carried himself in an unmistakably military way, back erect and movements clipped and deliberate. Handsome, too, she observed guiltily, his close-cropped silver hair suiting his chiselled looks.

He signalled to two of his subordinates, who slung their rifles over their shoulders and went over to the flier. Taking hold of one of the crates, the two men carefully lifted it from the low bed and carried it a short distance from the vehicle, before placing it gently on the ground.

They were less cautious with the second crate, swinging it casually from the flier and all but dropping it on the ground next to the first one. They opened the second crate first and pulled out a selection of all-in-one coveralls, in a clearly synthetic material that was a bright, warning yellow. They and the rest of the men started to pull the coveralls on over their clothes. The suits were hooded, covering the head, with a small, transparent face shield. The fastenings were complex, and the men started checking each other's to ensure they were on correctly.

"Shit, shit, shit..." muttered Aecola as she inched her way back up the slope to where Bokka was still hiding.

"Are they hazmat suits? What the hell is this? What were they talking about?"

"I don't know. They didn't refer directly to anything, just argued about whether or not this was the right spot for their mission, whatever it is. Talking about local flora, wind patterns, dispersal..."

"This is bad," said Bokka, her voice wavering.

Down in the clearing, the seven men were now fully kitted up in their protective suits. Carefully, two of the men, now indistinguishable but Aecola assumed the two civilians, opened the clasps on the first crate. Small clouds of vapour escaped as the crate was unsealed, suggesting the contents were being kept at a controlled, low temperature. Waving the vapour aside, one of them reached in and pulled out what at first glance looked like a misshapen Plomo-ball, about a foot in diameter and a mottled orange colour, as his colleague removed a sharp instrument the length of his forearm that tapered to a wicked-looking spike. The ball looked like some sort of... fungi?

Aecola's eyes widened. The colour drained from her face.

"Run!"

It was Petru who spotted the movement. The squad leader cursed the hazmat suits for muffling so much of the external noise, but the shaking of the bushes was unmissable.

"Movement, top of the ridge!" he yelled, pointing in the direction that Bokka and Aecola had been hiding in.

Jens Yoak was holding the fungus gingerly in both hands as his colleague Boll was wielding the spike. Both were distracted by the yelling and unfortunately for Yoak, it came right at the moment that Boll was about to make the incision into the first fungal ball. The amount Yoak shifted by was almost insignificant yet, with Boll also distracted, it was enough to cause the instrument to catch a glancing blow through Yoak's glove and into the fungus.

Yoak screamed as the fungus deflated, a plume of spores erupting from it. "My suit! My suit!" He didn't even feel the pain of the gash caused by the spike or see the blood. The only thing he saw was the tear in his suit. He dropped the deflated fungus and did the worst thing he could do; he grabbed his injured hand with the other glove, trying to seal the compromised suit. He couldn't have found a quicker way to ensure that the spores that had lightly sprayed out over his hands and chest found their way inside the tear.

Oblivious to all this, Petru and his squad were fully focused on whatever had been watching them. Two of his men opened fire on the ridge. The other two split up and started to ascend the slope either side of the target area.

"Captain Petru! Captain Petru!"

Petru turned around to face Boll, the question dying on his lips as he saw the sobbing, petrified Yoak sink to his knees, one bloody glove wrapped around the other. He cursed and ran over to the two scientists.

"What happened?" he yelled over the noise of his men shooting up the undergrowth. The buzz of the pulse rifles suddenly died as the two men firing lowered their weapons and set off to follow the two who had already ascended the ridge.

"I don't know!" yelled Boll in reply, oblivious to the fact that there was now no need for shouting.

"You stuck my hand! When you speared the ball, you stuck my hand! You tore my suit!" Yoak was in full panic, his mind overcome with terror.

"You were exposed?"

"I don't know!"

Petru swore. He wasn't sure what the hell had just gone wrong, but this was not supposed to have been in any way a difficult mission. Now, in a matter of just a few seconds, it looked like they'd been compromised and one of the scientists probably infected.

"Show me."

"No!" sobbed Yoak. "If I take my hand off, I'll expose the tear, then I won't have a chance!"

"He's right," said Boll, ashen-faced beneath the hood of his hazmat suit. "We need to get him to a medical facility immediately."

"How long before the infection becomes untreatable, if he has been exposed?"

"I don't know exactly. Hours, though, not days."

"Then we can't," replied Petru.

"What do you mean you can't?" sobbed Yoak.

"At this range, you estimated it will take three weeks for the fungus to establish securely and then spread as far as the nearest settlement. If we turn up at a medical facility with him like this, the local authorities would be alerted to the infection and the clear-up would start before we'd got anywhere."

"Are you sure?" asked Boll. "Couldn't you order them to keep it to themselves?"

"This is a black op," snapped Petru. "I've no authority to wield. And even if I did, we can't take the risk. It would only take one orderly with a big mouth... If it gets out that this was a deliberate act, we'll all be cut loose and likely shot."

"What if we just drop him off, leave him and clear out before we're questioned?"

"And rely on him not to say anything?"

"I... I... w... wouldn't..." Yoak was breathing heavily now, his panic response using up the oxygen within the confines of his suit. "I promise... I wouldn't..."

Petru ignored him, still looking at Boll. "Not a chance, doc."

"Well, wouldn't it be the warning we wanted? The end result's the same..."

"The end result is not the same. It's one thing to put the idea in people's heads, but if they know it was deliberately introduced to the environment then the changes in legislation the president is after become meaningless. Then Yoak will have died for nothing."

"Died? I... I'm not dead yet! It's treatable if we hurry!"

Petru pulled the bolt-pistol from the holster on his hip and fired once, putting a shot clean through Yoak's head, killing him instantly. Boll yelped and nearly jumped out of his skin.

"It was a kindness. We couldn't take him anywhere to be

treated and I wasn't about to let him die a slow painful death. I don't like it, Boll, but he was dead the moment *you* tore his suit."

Boll looked over at his colleague's body, lying prone on the clearing floor. Tears coursed down his face.

"We'll leave him here," continued Petru in a calmer tone. "By the time anyone comes looking, the fungus will have long consumed him. Get the other ball out and finish the job, Boll."

Boll ignored him, shaking now as he stared at Yoak's body.

Petru shook his head in exasperation, then raised his bolt-pistol again and held it to Boll's head.

"Now, Doctor Boll. The fungus."

Boll turned slowly towards the soldier and, after a moment, nodded and took a few tentative steps towards the crate.

Petru reached the top of the slope to find his men stood by the body of a young woman.

"Talk to me."

"She was dead when we got up here, must have been caught by a lucky shot from Jekk or Tyger from the clearing," replied Goff, Petru's second-in-command.

Zane, who was knelt next to the body, quickly reeled off what they had discovered. "Young woman, no more than twenty-two, twenty-three... No identification. Netaran, looking at the ink. She had a pack, but the contents are so much slag at this point, pulse must have gone right through it and got her in the back as she was running. Looks like there might have been a satellite uplink in there, judging by some of the remains, but honestly, that's a guess."

"So, we've no idea who she is or what she was doing here." Petru crouched by the body, reaching out a gloved hand to gently prod the remains of the backpack. "Or, if it was an uplink, whether she used it before running."

Zane held up his hands apologetically.

Jekk, who with Tyger had been sweeping the immediate area for any sign of further infiltrators, piped up. "This is prime territory for illegal logging camps. My guess is she was an eco-activist. They send them out here to monitor and report any illegal loggers, try to shut them down. Young kids like her, students. Would explain the comms gear too."

"Illegal log…?" Petru held up a hand. "Never mind. So, young do-gooder sees the flier, comes here for a closer look, expecting to find loggers and instead stumbles over us. Of all the luck." He closed his eyes for a moment, cursing to himself. "You know anything about these activists, Jekk? She likely to be on her own?"

Jekk ran a hand over his shaved head and shrugged. "Not much, chief, but I'd say probably not. They send them out for months at a time, so there must be at least two of them, for company and in case of emergency."

"Right. So, the question is, did her friend stay back at camp or were they here too?"

"And if she did already report what she saw?" asked Zane.

Petru thought for a moment before getting to his feet. "If the game's up, it's up, nothing we can do about it. But until we know otherwise, we proceed as if no contact was made."

"Captain Petru! Look at this."

Tyger was a short way off, poking his gun into the undergrowth.

"Looks like someone else *was* here. And left in an awful hurry…"

By mid-afternoon, Aecola was back in the tree house shaking, sitting on the floor with her back against the wall, her face wet with tears. She had let Bokka down, so badly. Her heart tore anew as she relived the moment her friend had cried out and fallen, face first, onto the forest floor, her backpack a smoking, charred mess, her back opened up, organs vaporized.

She'd tried to drag her, refusing to believe the obvious, that Bokka was dead, but she couldn't budge her. Then she tried to see if there was anything of use left in the backpack, thinking specifically of the satellite linkup, but it was clear that nothing remained. All the while as she was doing this, more shots from the soldiers' pulse rifles were buzzing around her, smashing into trees and bringing down branches.

Aecola had no idea how she'd made it back alive. The last few hours were a blur of panicked crashing through the undergrowth, interspersed with unbearably tense periods of trying to control her breathing as she hid, waiting for the sudden shouts and gun blasts that meant she had been discovered. Yet somehow, they never came. After what felt like an eternity, she arrived back at the place she and Bokka had called home for the past three months, the ropes they used for ascending to the platform still dangling where they'd left them. Exhausted as she was, she had scurried up them as fast as she could, pulling them up behind her, still fearful of pursuit. She then lay down on the platform, eyes glued to the forest floor beneath, waiting for the soldiers to appear.

They never did.

Now, she had finally allowed herself to relax, just the tiniest amount, and with that letting go, came a flood of tears. Bokka was dead. What was she going to tell the university? What was she going to tell *Bokka's parents?* She had only met them once, but they had been so nice to her and they were devoted to Bokka, their only daughter. This would devastate the kindly couple.

Beyond that, though, was the fear of what she'd seen, yet not believed. Surely it couldn't have been what she thought? The footage on her datapad was inconclusive; without getting it to the university and running it through an enhancement programme, she couldn't be one hundred per cent sure she had identified the fungi correctly. Yet the tentativeness with which the men had handled it and the way they had all so carefully suited up beforehand all suggested, in the strongest terms, that she wasn't mistaken.

She had to move. Though the platform was four hundred feet up in the canopy, it would be extreme stupidity to assume it couldn't be discovered from the ground. The observation posts were designed to watch from a distance, not with an expectation that loggers would ever show up right beneath them. Although anyone walking casually below would probably be oblivious to her presence, there were no casual hikers in the forest. The only people who were likely to come past would be looking for her and she did not in any way want to be found.

She weighed up her options. She had another three months on her rotation, but Bokka was being picked up in a couple of weeks. She had more than enough rations to hold out until then, especially now... now she was on her own. She could abandon the tree house and wait nearby for the rendezvous, get back to the university that way.

But Aecola was no experienced outdoorswoman. Even if she hadn't needed to avoid patrols of soldiers looking for her, a couple of weeks without the comfort and security of the tree house would be a big ask. The forest was home to relatively few large predators, but they did exist. Not to mention the fact that she would need to be ready to move at any point, so would need to have food enough for that time that she could carry easily without trying to live off the land. No, it was clear that, as a strategy, that would be beyond her.

Besides, if she was right about what she'd seen, she didn't have weeks. In that time, not only would the fungus have reached her tree house and beyond, but it would also have spread as far as the nearest town, Gran Palomos. It was a small community, just a few thousand residents, mainly indigenous peoples, but all in danger of infection by the time Bokka's pick-up was due. Aecola had to get word out before then.

That meant hiking. She would head for Gran Palomos. It was hardly close by, but she should be able to get there within five or six days. It meant going back in the direction of the soldiers though and the thought of that made her ill.

Then she had a brainwave. Still sat, she leaned over and reached into her pack and pulled out her datapad. There was no signal here, without the satellite linkup, but that was okay, she knew that what she was after was downloaded onto the pad itself. She pulled up a map of the area and... there! The next observation post. Just three days away and in the opposite direction, away from the soldiers. They'd have a working satellite uplink, she could transmit her data back to the university, alert the authorities, get Gran Palomos evacuated and get the hell out of the forest herself.

She grabbed a bigger pack and started organising what she should take.

Petru stepped out onto the platform and paused to marvel at the view. Quite aside from the ecological implications, it wasn't hard to sympathise with those who wanted to preserve this forest. The immense carpet of green spread out before him was truly beautiful. For a moment, he allowed himself regret that his mission was going to be the catalyst for devastation on a scale far greater than a handful of illegal logging operations. It was distasteful, to say the least, but Petru was a career soldier. He'd been given his orders and his personal feelings didn't come into it. Had he been ordered to do the same on his own world, he might have thought otherwise but... He swiftly buttoned down those feelings and stepped back inside the tree house.

"Well?"

Jekk was hunched over his console, which was hardwired into a satellite linkup. "Be a lot easier if we could get a regular signal out here," he muttered to himself.

Petru cleared his throat.

"Sorry, sir. The dead woman's name was Bokka Rumescu, she was a student at the University of Talos. Captain of their Plomo-ball squad. Looks like Talos U just lost their shot at the championship..."

"Jekk..."

The soldier held up his hand by way of an apology. "Checking local law enforcement records turned up nothing. Couple of notations in the university files, campus protests, nothing extraordinary. Eco causes, naturally..." Jekk continued his search. "No declared affiliations. Most of these kids wind up on the logging monitoring through sheer goodwill rather than any long-term connection to any one group. Like as not, she just saw a pamphlet on a noticeboard and decided to take a term off."

"Any indication who she was here with?" Petru tried to swallow his impatience. He knew, in all likelihood, that finding the information Jekk was looking for would be like finding a needle in a haystack. Rushing the soldier wouldn't get the info quicker but it was hard not to let his frustration over this ridiculous complication get the better of him. He glanced over at where Goff and the others were turning over the contents of the tree house, searching for any identifier. If the activist had any sense, they'd have taken anything that could ID them, but you never knew, in a panic...

"Wait, I might have something... I've been checking the sabbatical records."

"Sabbatical?"

Jekk turned to face Petru, removing his cap and scratching at his shaved scalp as he did so. "Several universities actively support these monitoring outfits. The kids don't drop out, they're granted a sabbatical. The student takes a few months off, their place is kept open for them by their university, so their studies aren't compromised. Anyways, Rumescu was put on sabbatical three months ago, so I ran a check on all students who were granted a break at the same time. There's one name here that cross matches; shared a few classes, written up for a couple of the same protests. Ecological ones."

"And?"

"Off-worlder, an Ekkaran."

Petru leaned over to peer at the console over Jekk's shoulder. There, staring back at him from the picture on her university registration, was Aecola.

II

Lukasz flopped down on the chair in Kinsey's office, swinging his dirty boots up onto the desk as he unthinkingly reached out a finger and pushed at Kinsey's favourite desk toy, sending the tiny spaceship whizzing round on its chain. He leaned forward slightly, adjusting his position to free the long hair at the back of his head that he'd trapped when he sat. The rest of his hair was cropped quite short, creating an unfashionable look that he doggedly stuck to, not helped by his somewhat ratty moustache. His clothes were faded, old and grubby; and as such he seemed to be a natural part of the faded, old and grubby office. It was darker inside than it should have been, several of the windows blocked with boxes and piles of paperwork, and there was a slightly unpleasant odour of oil and old sweat that permeated everything. He stared vacantly at the desk, not really seeing the things in front of him, thinking instead of the man who usually sat there.

"You okay?"

He looked up at Wiktoria. "Yeah, I guess." He slowly unfastened the mourning band from the sleeve of his battered old flight jacket and tossed it onto the desk. "It still doesn't seem real. I keep expecting him to walk through the door, coughing a lung up. I mean, I know he wasn't healthy, anyone could see that. But you still don't expect…"

"I know." Wiktoria removed her own mourning band. Unlike Lukasz, she had made the effort for Kinsey's internment, exchanging her usual electric blue catsuit for one in charcoal grey. Her blue braids were banded together, hanging down her back almost to her waist. Her sharp, angular features were knitted in an expression of concern as she looked over at the door, where Xin stood. They shrugged and tapped their fingers in a swift and deliberate pattern. Wiktoria nodded. "We're sorry, Lukasz, really. I liked the old boy, in his way."

Lukasz smiled softly, fingers stroking his downy moustache. "Yeah, he was okay. Treated me well enough, I guess."

"And he really left you this place?"

Lukasz spun slowly in the chair, looking round at the crappy, tiny office, with its precarious heaps of paperwork and scattered mechanical parts. He opened his arms wide, as if to encompass the immediate surroundings.

"Every last screw. I guess I'm slightly less poor trash now."

Wiktoria flashed him a quick grin. "Master of all you survey?"

"Something like." Lukasz pushed himself up from the chair. "Well, he didn't have any family and you can tell by the number of people who showed up this morning what state his friendships were in. I'm more surprised he'd gotten around to making a will than I am by the fact that mine was the only name he could think of to put in it. Shall we?"

He gestured at the second door. Wiktoria and Xin made to follow him as he stepped towards it and opened it wide.

The sun was at its zenith and Lukasz and Wiktoria instinctively raised their hands to shield their eyes from the glare as they stepped out of the dingy office. Xin pulled the hood of their black coat forward, throwing their face in shadow. Xin, naturally very pale, made a point of covering themselves as much as possible for protection from the harsh Tethrian sun. Beneath the sleeves of their long black coat, they wore long gloves with just the fingertips removed for tactility. The bottom half of their face was covered by a thin black scarf, leaving just their eyes visible, peering out from between locks of sandy hair.

The salvage yard was small by most standards. Their home was a backwater on Tethree, itself a remote system. Over the few acres that Kinsey... that Lukasz owned, a scattering of ships in various states of disrepair sat like sad islands in a dispiriting sea of rusting, broken parts.

"It's no small inheritance, to be fair," said Wiktoria. "Surely some of these ships must be close to flightworthy. A bit of hard work and you could find enough to sell to do what you want."

Lukasz rubbed at his chin. "Yeah. I mean, I won't see any cash for a while, but if I take a couple of guys on and manage to keep the yard going as a business while I carry out the work then yeah, you're right, we might be able to squeeze something out of it."

"We?"

Lukasz gave Wiktoria a playful punch on the arm. "You don't think I want to do this without you, do you?"

He looked back over Wiktoria's shoulder and winked at Xin, who raised their hands and tapped out a brief signal.

"See? Xin is up for it."

Wiktoria pulled a face. "Xin just wants to sit in old ships and spend their life tinkering away with obsolete computers. If you think I'm going to let you two idiots turn into a pair of Kinseys..."

"Lukasz Quilter?"

The three of them looked up in unison. A few metres from where they were stood, three men were looking at them through one of the yard's external gates. Two of them were strangers, serious men in anonymous suits with anonymous faces. One of them was carrying an attaché case under his arm. They were accompanied by Batson, the local sheriff.

Lukasz, his heart sinking, walked over and unlocked the gate.

This did not bode well.

"How much did they take?"

"Everything. They cleared me out."

Lukasz had finally caught up with Wiktoria and Xin in the dingy bar across the street from the yard. It was a week after Kinsey's internment and about an hour or so after the lunch-time rush. The bar was more or less deserted.

The government officials had been investigating Kinsey for months, it transpired, and were just about to launch their case when the old man had had his stroke and died. Several years of underdeclared tax and off-the-books work, all reported by one of his clients. No doubt some chickenshit that had been caught themselves and offered Kinsey up in return for a lighter penalty. Maybe Kinsey had gotten wind of it, it might even have been a contributary factor in his death, who knew? He'd certainly been in a weird mood for a couple of months. Or so Lukasz thought in retrospect, before dismissing the idea. It was easy to start seeing signs where none existed and none of it made the slightest bit of difference. The government had too much evidence to even think about contesting it and within a couple of hours of Lukasz first opening the gate to them, the trucks had started arriving. Assessors had started moving through the yard and every bit of scrap in the place was tagged, bagged and, where possible, shipped out.

It had taken a few days but, in the end, they had removed all but the largest of the ships. The acres of yard now sat mainly empty, a few small heaps of the most useless parts scattered here and there. They had left Lukasz the yard, the land itself being of little value.

"The only consolation is that they have officially wiped the debt," said Lukasz, raising a finger to catch the attention of the bartender. He waited as his drink was poured and placed in front of him, then knocked the bar once with the glass before upending it and taking the shot down in one go. "I was convinced they were going to leave me a company with substantial debts. I'd be working for years just to pay them off." He snorted. "Guess they figured that was a bad job."

"So, you'll be making money from now, at least."

Lukasz let out a brief, humourless laugh. "No chance. Without the stock, I really would be starting from scratch, and right now I don't have the cash to buy a smashed-up desert skipper. I've got nothing to start up with." He drew a finger through a pool of spilt liquor on the bar and traced a small circle, round and round. "No, my only option is to sell the land, which by the way is practically worthless, and get a job."

Xin started to waggle their fingers, but Wiktoria reached over and placed a hand gently on their wrist, shaking her head. Lukasz ordered another round for the three of them and when it arrived, again, knocked his back in one.

"You can stick a fork in me, I'm done."

It was twilight when they left the bar. The sun had sunk behind the mountains to the east and the street lighting was starting to glow. Lukasz stood, swaying slightly, out the front of the bar, looking across the dirt road at the salvage yard he'd briefly owned. *Damn you, Kinsey, did you know this was coming? Did you know this all wasn't worth shit when you left it to me?* He shook his head to try and clear the fuzziness.

"Come on."

He led them unsteadily across the road and they spent a few minutes shivering slightly as Lukasz fumbled with his key chain to let them in. He let the gate swing open behind them as he stumbled into the yard.

There were just three ships left in the yard, all tagged and secured, waiting for the tax inspectorate to find big enough transports to get the grounded spaceships out. Lukasz trailed his hand along the hull of one as the three wandered aimlessly in the empty yard. "I oughta…" Lukasz interrupted himself with a meaty belch. "I oughta charge them storage while the ships remain here."

Xin started to move their fingers, but they didn't seem to be working quite as they should. They gave up and, in slight, whispering tones, said, "Are you gonna?"

Lukasz stopped in his tracks, swaying gently from side to side as he considered the idea. "I should, you know." Then he pushed himself on and started ambling again. "Nah, wouldn't do me any favours. Need them to forget about this place as soon as possible."

The three wandered aimlessly for a while, passing a bottle between them and reminiscing about Kinsey, reliving stories about growing up under the old man's eye, stopping occasionally for Lukasz to kick at a pile of junk.

"What's that?"

They were now in one of the furthest corners of the yard and Wiktoria was pointing at something that had started to loom out of the darkness, a sizeable something.

"Hmm," said Lukasz, surprised. "Looks like they missed one."

The three made their way over to the something which, as

they got closer, coalesced into the shape of a small freighter.

"Well, I'll be…"

The battered ship was in a bad state. Multiple signs of botched repair jobs showed plainly even from the outside, different coloured panels where replacements had been scrounged and slapped on. As he came to a stop in front of it, Lukasz tentatively reached out his hand, as if afraid it would vanish the moment he tried to touch it.

In the dim twilight, with the drink still making it slightly difficult to focus, he didn't readily recognise the ship. "I'm not even sure I knew this was here."

"But the g-men must have seen it, yeah? I mean they weren't just going by Kinsey's books; they were physically cataloguing everything within the fence, right?" said Wiktoria, looking at Lukasz.

He nodded. "Absolutely. Whatever it is, I guess they didn't want it." He squinted and, in a confused tone to himself, said, "I don't even know *what* this is…"

"Maybe," Xin whispered, "it's your way out."

The side door to the ship was jammed, beyond the capabilities of three drunks to force it open. But Lukasz eventually managed, with the help of a discarded bracing strut he found in a pile of unclaimed trash a few metres away, to prise open the rear cargo ramp, just enough to pull himself up and into the cargo bay. The ship had no power but with the strut, from the inside, he was able to push the ramp open further, allowing Wiktoria and Xin up behind him.

Lukasz unclipped the flashlight from his belt and used it to illuminate the inside of the cargo bay. There were ladders either side of the bay, leading up to gantries that themselves led into the ship's interior. A few crates, open and empty, were scattered around the deck. Lukasz kicked a few over, looking for anything useful or valuable.

"Not a sausage," he giggled. He looked up, flashing his light along the gantries, trying to find anything that might identify the vessel, or even its class.

Meanwhile, Wiktoria had walked over to a doorway at the far end of the hold. "Lukasz, bring the flashlight."

He went to where she was standing, peering through the doorway into a short corridor.

"Whassat?"

She took the flashlight from him and led the way. The corridor opened out into what looked like a second hold.

"What the hell...?"

The room was smaller than the main cargo bay and almost completely empty, which would have argued the case for it just being more storage, except in the centre of the room were the remains of what looked like a large glass tank. The tank had been shattered and broken glass lay all over the floor. The whole room looked dirty, dirtier than the cargo bay, decades-old stains on the floor and...

"Oh shit!"

They both jumped as a sweep of the flashlight illuminated what looked like bones on the floor. Human bones.

"What happened in here?" murmured Wiktoria as she knelt to examine the bones. It was impossible to tell how the person had died but she started to sober up quickly as she realised that the skeleton wasn't complete.

Xin appeared in the doorway, stepping into the room and starting to walk around. After a moment, they turned and signalled to Lukasz, drawing his attention to a battered, rusty gurney in one corner. Lukasz shrugged. This was super creepy and none of it made a lick of sense.

"I'm guessing the tank is some kind of water storage?" he said.

Wiktoria rolled her eyes. "For someone who works with old spaceships, you don't know a lot about old spaceships. That's an interface."

"A what now?"

She stood and walked over to the remains of the tank. "An interface. You know, from before the Heisen Breakthrough?"

Lukasz looked at her blankly.

She sighed. "A hundred or so years ago, Milos Heisen decoded the route to hollow space, opening the door to fully automated FTL travel. Prior to that, the only way to access it was via an Interface. Pilots were submerged into a quasi-sentient, viscous bioform, held in tanks like this one." She stepped gingerly into the tank and reached up, taking hold of an array of cables dangling from the ceiling. "The pilot would have been connected to the flight drive via these cables, applied directly to the base of the brain stem."

"What the hell?"

"It was barbaric, yes, but it was the only way to achieve FTL," Wiktoria shrugged. "Being a pilot was a one-way gig. Once in the tank, that was that. Taking you out would kill you. Invariably they went insane, but the biological combination of the gloop and the human brain was the only way of cracking the maths needed."

"Why would anyone agree to that?"

"Not all of them did," said Wiktoria as she reached out to place a hand gently on the wall of the tank. "Convicts, lifers, were often used. Then you had those trying to lift their families out of insurmountable debt and some who were press-ganged into it. Then you had the handful of drug-addled hippies who hoped it would open their minds to the mysteries of the universe." She turned back and looked at Lukasz, quizzically. "You really didn't know any of this?"

Lukasz shook his head. "I scrap 'em, I don't study 'em. And frankly, I don't think I ever saw one this old before. I certainly had no idea this was here."

"Well, it explains why the government goons left it. This, my friend, is an interstellar ship incapable of interstellar flight." She stepped out of the tank again and handed the flashlight back to Lukasz. "This here is worthless."

III

Lukasz slept at the yard. There was a cot in the office, and he couldn't face going home. In fact, when it came to it, he pretty much passed straight out the moment he lay down, so whether he would have made it home in any event was debatable. The next morning, when he woke up, his head was pounding. He pulled an errant lock of hair from his mouth and rolled over. His flight jacket that had lain across him like a blanket fell to the floor as he did so. Lying on his back, he tried not to move his head or acknowledge to himself the funky smell that filled the office and which, he was sure, was emanating from himself. He also tried to ignore the taste of... what was that? in his mouth. The night before was a blur and he was too muddle-headed to try and pick the pieces apart.

Around midday, as he still lay prone on the cot, Wiktoria and Xin banged on the door and let themselves in. Xin slumped into the chair behind the desk and started spinning themselves around in it. Wiktoria dropped a packet wrapped in foil onto Lukasz's chest before grabbing a hold of his legs and swinging them around so she could perch on the cot next to him.

"Guessing you've not eaten yet."

"You guess right." Lukasz unwrapped the packet to find a steaming lun wrap. "Man, that smells good." Still horizontal with his legs hanging off the cot, he tore a huge bite from it and started to chew, mumbling something unintelligible through a mouthful of wrap as bits of food dropped onto his chest.

"Manners," said Wiktoria.

He chewed and swallowed, before saying again, "How are

you two so active this morning? I feel like hell."

"I think you overestimate how much we were keeping up with you last night." Wiktoria sighed and reached over, plucking a strand of something from the wrap that had caught itself in Lukasz's moustache.

Xin brought themselves to a halt and fingered something at Lukasz, getting just a single finger in return.

"My mouth tastes like something died in it." Lukasz took another huge bite of wrap.

"Xin has been thinking. You want to take another look at that old freighter?"

"Sure, just give me a moment to finish this."

It was somewhat more than a moment before Lukasz felt recovered enough to drag himself out of the cot and as he stepped out into the bright sunlight, he suddenly felt overcome by nausea. He ran around the side of the cabin to throw up. Reappearing, he wiped his mouth, pulled a battered pair of tinted glasses from his pocket and put them on. Wiktoria, who'd clearly been expecting something of the like, reached into her bag and took out another wrap, chucking it over to him. "Try to keep this one down, sailor." Lukasz pulled a face.

They started walking to the freighter. "I don't remember it being this much of a hike last night," muttered Lukasz.

"I'm surprised you remember it at all, frankly. You put quite a bit away."

"I just buried my friend and had my inheritance confiscated; I think I have a right to be feeling sorry for myself."

"Hey, I'm not saying you don't," replied Wiktoria, her hands raised in a pacifying gesture.

They walked the rest of the way in silence, Lukasz sipping periodically from the water bottle Wiktoria had also thoughtfully provided.

As they got nearer, they got their first sight of the ship in daylight. "Shiiit," muttered Lukasz to himself, "Ship looks worse than I do."

"There's hull repair needed," observed Wiktoria straightaway. Of the three, despite Lukasz's experience in scrap, she probably had the most mechanical aptitude. If they ever stood a chance of getting the ship spaceworthy again, Lukasz hoped he could convince her to come along as engineer.

"No doubt. It'd be amazing if there wasn't, given how old she is. Are those cannons underneath?" he asked, raising his tinted glasses for a better look.

Wiktoria frowned. "Shouldn't be. I had a read around last night; I think it's a Tataryn class. No armaments."

They got closer and finally stopped by the hull. Sure enough, a pair of cannons had been slung underneath. Wiktoria stepped under the hull for a closer look.

"Not standard, these have been added on. Not very professionally either."

"Cool," said Lukasz. "You think I got myself a pirate ship?"

Wiktoria grinned at him. "I think maybe you do."

They took a once around the outside. "Okay, so there are two or three areas that need new panels, the rest of the hull repairs should be straightforward. I think it's just decay, I don't see any signs of significant damage."

The cargo ramp was still ajar from where Lukasz had forced it open the night before. The three pulled themselves up and, once more, stood in the hold.

"See if you can't open that ramp properly, get as much natural light in here as possible," instructed Wiktoria.

Lukasz complied automatically. If this was an inspection with a view to making the ship spaceworthy then, regardless of ownership, this was Wiktoria's gig. Personally, he didn't think there was any chance of getting her flying again but, hell, he didn't have anything better to do today...

It was certainly less eerie with daylight streaming in. Not any more encouraging, but less eerie. The hold didn't yield anything more exciting than they'd found the night before. A few empty crates and some tool racks, stripped of their tools. There was an outside chance, Lukasz realised, that some of them might be the same tools he'd been using for years. It could easily have been here in the yard that the ship was cleared out. Kinsey wasn't one to leave anything of value in any of his acquisitions.

They climbed up to the gantry and carried out a quick sweep

of the upper decks, with the aid of a set of Lukasz's standing lights that Xin had collected on the way to the yard. Thankfully, Lukasz had a basic set of his own tools that weren't listed under the company assets, which he kept in a local lock-up. Working on ships with no power was commonplace so good portable lighting was essential. Lukasz's basic kit created enough light to be tolerable.

The three of them were taken aback by the signs of what looked like a firefight in the living area. Scorch marks along the corridors and the galley at the end was a mess. Whatever had taken place on the old freighter, presumably someone had got the ship flying again for it to have made it into Kinsey's hands. But if that was the case, it hadn't been for long, as there was no sign that any cleaning up had occurred. The cabins looked reasonable, though, and the three made their way up to the flight deck.

"I would love to know what this old girl's story is," said Wiktoria, running a finger through the dust on the pilot's seat, as much to herself as to Lukasz and Xin.

"I still don't see how we're going to get this heap flying."

"Ever the optimist." Wiktoria pulled a hairband from her pocket and secured her blue plaits before lowering herself under the primary flight console. With not too much difficulty, she managed to prize the panel off and get to the circuitry beneath. "Xin, Lukasz is bumming me out. Take him down to the front hold and tell him what you're thinking."

Xin nodded and turned around, heading off back to the cargo hold. Lukasz followed, shaking his head.

They climbed back down into the hold and from there into the front section with the glass tank. Lukasz activated another light, throwing the front compartment into sharp relief. He was thankful for the bluish tinge to the light as it was obvious that a lot of the stains on the floor were directly related to the partial skeleton. Xin crouched down by the bones and picked up the skull, studying it for a moment before standing again and respectfully resting it on a ledge that ran around the wall at head height. Then they stepped into the glass tank and turned to face Lukasz, their fingers moving in a blur.

"Woah, hold on," Lukasz raised his hands. "Take it slowly,

buddy, you know I'm not as quick as Wiktoria."

Xin signalled an apology and started again, slowing the movement of their fingers to accommodate Lukasz's hangover. Their plan was actually fairly straightforward. With a small amount of work, the cabling for the interface could be used to hook up a standard navi-computer down here, which would plug into the flight console in the same way, bypassing the need to reconfigure the whole flight deck. Xin was a tinkerer. They kept a lot of computer equipment in the apartment from which they also ran a small business, helping locals with their computing requirements. There were few programming issues that Xin couldn't handle; running a navi-computer should be straightforward, after a certain amount of research.

"And how much is this going to cost me? You know I was cleaned out."

"That's the beautiful part," said Wiktoria, appearing behind them as Xin folded their arms and fixed Lukasz with an unreadable stare. "You didn't think we'd be letting you fly off this rock on your own, did you?"

"Seriously?"

"Look, Lukasz, there's nothing keeping any of us here. Xin's parents kicked them out years ago, and I'm under no obligation from the order to remain at the mission. Tethree's a backwater, a dump. We've got nobody here except each other. This ship is our ticket out of here. We pick up a little freight here and there, we get out of here, see the galaxy. Xin and I talked it over last night when we left you. We've got assets... well, Xin has. Computer equipment they can offload, the bits we don't need ourselves, and they have work coming in they can do around the refit, earn whatever extra we need. We'll buy into the ship, as partners, split the profits, live the life we always talked about. You want to deal scrap for the rest of your days until you have your own stroke and die?"

Lukasz lowered himself to the floor, resting his back against the wall. The past few days had been a rollercoaster and on top of which he was still foggy from the night before. He tried to swallow down the emotions threatening to overwhelm him, taking a long pull on his water bottle to hide the moment.

"I won't lie, I had been hoping you'd feel like that," he finally said.

Xin waggled their fingers.

"Yeah, both of you. I'm no match for Wiktoria as an engineer but that's nothing compared to the yawning gulf between your programming abilities and mine. Of course, I want you along as well, buddy."

Xin bowed their head slightly, their straggly hair covering their face. It looked like Lukasz wasn't the only one feeling emotional at the thought of blowing the dust of Tethree off their feet.

"And you really think you can get her flying again?"

Wiktoria pursed her lips. "I'm... seventy per cent sure? I don't know, Lukasz, she's in one hell of a state of disrepair. But honestly, I don't think there's anything here that can't be fixed. At least, not enough to stop us getting off Tethree and starting working. We patch her up and get her running, we can finish her off as we go. The way I see it, what have we got to lose?"

The answer to that, of course, was nothing. Literally, almost, nothing. Xin gave up the rental on their apartment and moved into the yard with Lukasz. They borrowed a crawler from one of Kinsey's old contacts and spent a few sweaty hours dragging the ship from its resting place to where the offices stood, to make the overhaul easier. Xin carted all their computing equipment and spares over, transforming the office into a makeshift workshop, out of which they continued to take jobs in between working on the ship, to cover the costs as best they could. Wiktoria wound up her commitments and joined them at the yard a few days later. It was her idea to get the cabins ready for living first, by way of a quick win that would also afford them more room to spread out. That way Xin could use all the offices, and they would also start to feel more of a crew and invested in the ship as they bunked in her. She didn't mention it, but it also meant she didn't have to share a disgusting office with them.

Power was restored to the ship fairly easily and the hull breaches were quickly patched too. The engine and internal systems proved trickier, but Wiktoria's instincts had been on the money. None of the problems they found were insurmountable and though money was tight, the three of them pooled their reserves and that, together with Xin's income, took them to their first test flight in just ten weeks.

A week or so before that first flight was scheduled, Wiktoria took a few days off and went away to visit her order. She returned in the Mission's skimmer with Erkon, one of the brothers from the mission. Erkon was a jovial older man, muscular but with a prodigious belly and sparse wispy hair.

"Lukasz! Long time!" he bellowed as he brought the skimmer to a halt in the shadow of the freighter.

Lukasz was sat on the cargo ramp, shirtless and pulling on a beer bottle, taking a break from his morning's work. He stood up and grinned at the newcomer.

"Erkon, they still let you drive that thing?"

Erkon laughed, a rich hearty bark of a laugh. Easing his bulk over the side of the skimmer, he held his arms open and embraced Lukasz, almost squeezing the life out of him.

"Woah, hold on there, Erkon. Breathing here."

Erkon let Lukasz go and instead took the younger man's shoulders in his hands, his iron grip also making Lukasz wince slightly.

"I was sorry to hear about the old man, Lukasz. He was a grouchy old bastard, but I was fond of him. We held a ceremony for him up at the mission."

"He would have hated that," smiled Lukasz ruefully.

"Why do you think we did it?" Erkon barked with laughter again, letting go of Lukasz with a final, stinging clap on his shoulders.

Lukasz peered over Erkon's shoulder at the rear of the skimmer, which was laden with small crates. "So, what's all this?"

"The order have a little going-away present for us," replied Wiktoria, grabbing one of the crates and thrusting it into Lukasz's arms. "You might want to get these loaded."

The three of them made light work of the crates and, when they were stowed in the hold, Lukasz opened one. It was packed full of supplies, food mainly.

"The best array of dried, reconstituted almost-food. Enough there to keep the three of you going for a couple of months. We figured if you were starting up your own trading company, you might be light on these kinds of resources. You need to eat while you're earning that first million credits."

Lukasz was, for a moment, speechless. "This is very kind."

Erkon waved aside his gratitude. "You're taking one of our own as your crew, we had to look out for her. Besides, consider it an advance on your first fee."

Lukasz raised his eyebrows.

"There's a mission on Altros-3, recently settled," said Wiktoria. "They're in desperate need of supplies and if the test flight's successful, the order are willing to employ our services."

"I assume we'll get a hefty discount in return for our support," winked Erkon. "Ah, here they are. Xin! I wondered where you were."

Xin had appeared from the ship's interior. They held up a hand in greeting to Erkon and signalled a brief message, which Erkon returned in kind.

"I understand your navigator's had their work cut out for them."

"We all have," said Wiktoria, "but yeah, Xin has had quite the complex task. You nearly done?"

With an uncharacteristic flourish, Xin extended their arm and indicated that the three of them should follow them.

The front hold had, like much of the ship, undergone an extensive remodelling. Scrubbed and polished, and now with proper lighting, the room could have been almost welcoming, except Xin had, to Lukasz's consternation, refused to throw out the skull with the rest of the bones they'd found. Instead, it sat in pride of place on the ledge where they had first placed it, a pair of small green bulbs installed in its eyes and wired up. The thing was ghoulish, in Lukasz's opinion, but Xin had always had a rather eldritch side.

The glass tank, where possible, had been saved; the broken edges heated and remoulded to form what Xin now referred to as their nest. Within the nest, they had attached a bank of computers to the cables that hung down from the ceiling. Lukasz had wanted to rip the whole thing out and see if they could maybe even rewire back to the cockpit and install the navi-computer there. But Xin had taken a liking to the hold and insisted that they would install themselves there. They had, in their downtime, even started decorating the walls of the hold with a bizarre mural, a quasi-abstract lurid mix of colours and shapes from which the forms of certain dark creatures could be made out. Frankly, it gave Lukasz the jitters and part of him suspected this was deliberate. A ploy to minimise the amount of time anyone else would want to spend there, giving the reclusive Xin the space they desired.

"This is quite the lair you've created for yourself," said Erkon. Xin nodded.

After Lukasz had given Erkon a brief tour of the rest of the ship, they all left and went down to the skimmer, where Erkon retrieved a small bag from behind the driver's seat. From the bag, he pulled out four bottles which he passed around, before cracking open his own. He raised it, to toast the new venture, then paused.

"What's she called?"

For a moment, nobody answered. Then Lukasz sheepishly spoke up. "I haven't registered her yet, was going to submit the forms after the test flight. Truth is, I haven't named her yet. I think I didn't want to jinx it by getting too attached too early."

"Ship needs a name, Lukasz," said Erkon. "You gotta open your heart to her sooner or later. And she might take offence if you start flying her before you've named her."

"I didn't have you down as a romantic, Erkon," smirked Wiktoria.

Erkon's face grew serious. "I'm only half-kidding. I'm not a superstitious man by nature, Wiktoria, but there's something not right about taking off in an unnamed ship. I assume she wasn't already registered, from before?"

Wiktoria shook her head. "We checked every serial number we could find. They don't all match," she said wryly. "It looks like there *might* have been some... creative record-keeping in her past. In any event, not a trace of her. Given how old she is, I'm not surprised."

"And nothing on her that hints at it?"

"There was something on the hull at one point, but it's worn away. An 'I', or maybe an 'L', and a 'J'. Not enough to make out though."

"There you are then, she's your baby to name."

Lukasz rubbed his nose. "I'm no good at this sort of thing. Wiktoria?"

"Oh no, Captain. She's your bird, that's your job."

Lukasz felt something tingle inside him. It was the first time she'd called him Captain. Even more than naming the ship, *that* suddenly made this all seem real.

"I'm not toasting her without a name..." said Erkon, his bottle still held high.

"The *Farewell to Tethree*," blurted out Lukasz.

"The *Farewell to Tethree*," chorused Wiktoria and Erkon, and the four of them clinked their bottles together and drank.

IV

Lukasz toggled a bank of switches and looked over to the display on his left to check the gauges were responding appropriately, then hit the intercom.

"Wiktoria? We're all good in the cockpit, how are you down there?"

"Engine's a go, Captain. She's warmed up and ready to fly."

"Xin, navigation?"

An eerie electronic voice sounded over the intercom. *"Ready."*

"Damn that synth voice," grunted Lukasz to himself. Xin had, after some forthright discussion, accepted that they would have to put aside their vocal reticence for the three of them to operate smoothly as a crew. After Wiktoria had repaired the comms system, though, the navigator had modified their headset to include a vocal distortion that stopped Xin hearing their own voice over the intercom. The synthetic voice that had resulted was, in Lukasz's mind, downright creepy.

"Okay people, this is it. The in-atmos tests were successful, we're ready to take her out in the deep sea now. Xin's programmed in a short flight to the Traikker system, where we'll emerge from hollow space and then return. The *Farewell* is logged for the trip, so this should be nice and straightforward."

"We all know what we're doing, Captain," replied Wiktoria.

"Well excuse me, some of us are trying to be professional," muttered Lukasz, scowling slightly. He leaned over and brought the engines up to temp and then, with the smallest of jolts, he took her up.

The thrill of flying again almost overwhelmed him, as he saw the ground fall away. The town and surrounding area that he'd spent his entire life in, shrank in his view as the ship ascended; the wider region becoming visible before it, too, started shrinking. Within a few minutes, they were at the outer limits of the atmosphere. Looking down on the planet, for the first time Lukasz thought it looked almost beautiful. It may be a dusty old hole but from up here, it shone. He let his gaze slide away from the planet and looked instead out at the stars, the inky black that, if all went well, would be his new home. It looked just as beautiful. He raised his hand and wiped something from his eye.

"Hull integrity is stable, no pressure on the life support," he announced.

"Everything down in the engine room is good, we're coasting."

"Okay, Xin, we're in your hands now. Let's see what you've been able to do."

"*Acknowledged. Hollow in five, four, three...*"

Lukasz's heart was in his mouth. It didn't help that the countdown sounded like it was coming from a computer rather than a living being. In the absence of being able to see his navigator, a human voice would have made him feel more comfortable.

"*... two, one...*"

Lukasz had seen hundreds of ships make the jump on videocasts, but nothing could prepare him for actually being onboard when a ship made the transition from real space to hollow space. The stars outside the cabin seemed to twist and fall away, seemingly taking his stomach with them as they spiralled out of view. "It's beautiful..." he whispered. Relieved of any activity during the journey through hollow space, Lukasz just leant back in his chair and watched the mysterious patterns of unreal light flicker and flow across the viewscreen. After a few minutes, Wiktoria appeared on the flight deck and took the co-pilot's seat. She looked over at Lukasz and the two shared a smile, but neither of them spoke. There was a profundity to the experience that neither of them wanted to break.

Instead, she reached over, took Lukasz's hand and the two of them just sat there, colours they'd never seen before flickering over the viewscreen, bathing them in an utterly unfamiliar glow.

The jump into hollow space was brief, the systems not too distant, and before long it was time to jump back into real space. Xin signalled the countdown to the return jump.

On the console to Lukasz's left, a warning light suddenly flashed, accompanied by a low, persistent buzzing.

"Xin, what's happening?"

Before they could respond, the ship seemed to lurch, causing Lukasz's stomach to make the reverse journey upwards again. The stars reappeared, jerking violently into existence.

"We're out!" Lukasz yelped into the intercom, taking hold of the controls.

The ship lurched again. A proximity alarm Lukasz didn't even know was functional started sounding.

"*Navigation error, ship not in expected zone.*"

"No shit!" yelled Lukasz.

The ship yawed heavily to one side and Lukasz almost screamed as the green horizon of a far-too-close planet lunged into view.

"Strap in! We've come out in Traikker's gravity well, I'm trying to pull up, but..."

An ominous groaning echoed through the ship.

Between the groaning of the ship and the proximity alarm's urgent wail, Wiktoria's voice was barely audible over the intercom. "...engine's struggling, Captain, ...think ...pull's too much!"

"Okay, I'm taking her down. Brace for impact, I've no idea what's down there!"

The front viewing monitor lit up as the ship lurched into the planet's atmosphere, a foreboding red glow licking at the sides of the screen. The ship fell into and out of clouds rapidly, the hull creaking and shuddering, before emerging above a forest. A huge, unending forest, with no sign of any settlement. Lukasz finally found the controls for the proximity alarm and shut the incessant wailing down. "I can't see any landing facilities! We seem to be coming down in wilderness! I don't know if I can land her!"

"You can do it, Lukasz!" Wiktoria's voice sounded surprisingly calm over the intercom. "I trust you! The hull will hold, just bring her down!"

"I wish I had your confidence," Lukasz muttered under his breath as the ship sped downwards. Blinking away the sweat that was stinging his eyes, he managed to get some traction on the stick, pulling her nose up slightly. "There you go, easy girl... Work with me here..."

The ground was still approaching too fast. The shaking was growing worse. There was an ominous kick as the ship breached the canopy, tearing its way through branches and trunks. "Hold on, girl, you're stronger than wood..."

Lukasz could see nothing now. All he could do was hold on to the stick and pray. Then came the jolt of the ship hitting the ground. There was a long, dreadful shriek of metal as the *Farewell to Tethree* tore a scar into the planet's surface. For what seemed like minutes all Lukasz could hear was the sound of stressed metal and trees being ploughed up outside before, with a final dreadful groan, the ship lurched to a stop.

Lukasz blacked out.

V

.

Aecola emerged from the stream and reached for her clothes. Two days on the run and it already felt like it had been a lifetime. Even after her perfunctory morning wash, she felt grimy all over. Slipping into her vest top, she picked up a band from the pile of clothes, reached back and tied her still-wet hair into a messy ponytail. She then pulled a protein snack from her bag and tore the corner of the wrapper off with her teeth, telling herself that it was a good job none of her classmates could see her spit the small corner of plastic into the undergrowth. It didn't take long for desperate circumstances to make you oblivious to niceties. She took a big bite of the snack and started chewing as she crouched down on her haunches, firing up her datapad and hoping against hope that there would now be a signal.

Nothing. She wasn't surprised, or even that disappointed. She knew it wasn't going to happen but there was always that small part of her that hoped, each time she looked at it, for the signal bar to suddenly register.

Oh well. She accessed the map and calculated her current position. She really wasn't that far now, just a few hours' hiking this morning and she should be at the next outpost. She hurriedly finished the snack, rammed the empty wrapper into her pack (there were limits) and pulled on her trousers and boots. It was a cool morning in the forest, but she knew that once she got started, she would warm up, so she left her jacket in the pack. She tied a bandana around her forehead, picked up her pack and started off.

Sure enough, it didn't take long for her to work up a sweat, despite the moderate temperatures. Aecola wasn't fond of sports, but she did keep herself fit. The gravity on Netaris was a fraction stronger than on Ekkaris so, like all the students from her home planet, she had taken to a regular fitness regime when she arrived, to allow her to compensate without undue stress. She'd been consistent with hers and had now reached a level of fitness she'd never had at home, gravity differences aside, so she had made good time on her trek.

Against all odds, she'd also started enjoying it. The forest was beautiful and as much as she'd been aware of that as she'd watched it from her tree house for the past three months, these two days of hiking through it had reinforced that impression in new ways. The way the sunlight filtered through the canopy, giving the light a soft, greenish tinge; the variety in flora she'd found as she moved further away from her basecamp; the occasional interaction with wildlife, when she'd come across a small deer drinking at a stream, or been chattered at by small, unseen tree-dwelling mammals who resented her encroachment into their territory. It was a whole new experience to being sat up in the canopy day after day with her eyes glued to her binocs. She had grown far more conscious of the earth beneath her feet.

She had been ascending slightly pretty much all the way from her starting point. Not in a way that was too exhausting, but it had certainly started to show in the type of undergrowth she was walking through. She was making better time now as the thicker brambles that grew in her area were thinning out, with more natural clearings appearing. Every now and then, she checked the internal compass on her datapad and reassured herself that she was heading in the right direction.

There had been no sign of pursuit. Aecola had been wary the first day, stopping periodically for minutes at a time, her ears straining for the slightest indication of other humans in the vicinity. By now, however, she reasoned that if she had been being followed, it was by someone with such skill that they were undetectable. If that were the case, there was no reason why she wouldn't have been apprehended before now anyway, so the only reasonable conclusion to be drawn was that she was alone. Maybe the soldiers had returned to their base of operations, either for backup or medical assistance. She held out little hope that they would have just assumed Bokka was alone. They would have found Bokka's body and, once they'd done that, her own trail would have been obvious, she was sure. She'd been more careful since leaving the tree house, but her initial flight from the scene had been driven by terror, not forethought. Only military protocol would have slowed them up enough to allow her to make a break for it. How far behind her they were now, she had no idea, but as long as they were out of sight, they could remain relatively out of mind.

She stopped in a clearing and pulled out her water bottle, taking a long swig and allowing herself a little to dampen her face. As she was putting it back, she froze. Somewhere nearby, something was moving through the forest, coming closer. Not from the direction that she had come, but nevertheless...

As quietly as she could, Aecola slipped behind a tree on the edge of the clearing and crouched down, trying to control her breathing, her heart pounding. Panic wouldn't help her. *Stay calm, stay still*. She listened.

There were voices now, the conversation unintelligible at the moment, but undoubtedly human voices. Aecola's throat tightened, and her stomach turned. *Please don't let it be them.* She closed her eyes for a moment, focusing on nothing other than the flow of her breath in and out of her lungs, keeping it slow and steady. Then she opened her eyes again and risked a peek from behind her tree. In the entire time she'd been out here, she'd not so much as set eyes on a single person other than Bokka but she knew there were still some indigenous tribes living out in the forest. With any luck, it was a hunting party. They might even be able to help her. She couldn't see anything yet, but the voices were getting louder...

"... saying is that this is a waste of time. Without our uplink, we can't achieve anything. We should admit defeat, wait for the pick-up and get out of here."

"The pick-up isn't until tomorrow. We're still on the clock and we can still record any activity to report later. It's not like any data we submit is time-critical anyway. We see what it's about and report it to the Enviro-subcommittee when we get back."

It's the team from the outpost! Aecola could have wept. Such was her relief that she didn't even register what the voice had said about having no uplink.

"It wasn't even a regular landing. Looked more like a crash to me."

"All the more reason we should go check it out. They might need help. You just don't want to make the effort."

Aecola was about to stand up when the thought crossed her mind that the conversation might be for her benefit, a trick to lure her out. She waited a few moments, until the owners of the two voices came into view, when her heart nearly burst. She recognised one of the two young men that entered the clearing, still arguing.

"Caden!" She stood up and called out to them.

One of the two, the shorter, plumper one, shrieked and actually jumped a few inches into the air. The taller one, Caden, didn't react quite so violently, but nevertheless, grabbed his chest with one hand and reached out to his friend with the other.

"Aecola?" Caden swore, vociferously. "You scared the hell out of us! What were you thinking, jumping out like that?"

Aecola's only response was to run across the clearing and throw her arms around her fellow student, sobbing.

"I don't understand. You're saying it was an Eschatonus spore?"

"Bullshit," scoffed Litton, Caden's partner. "For one thing, how would you know that? It's not like you could have ever seen one."

"Not in the flesh, no," admitted Aecola. "But I took a module on aggressive xeno-flora last semester, so I've seen the visual records from infected planets. I'm sure that's what it was. Maybe not one hundred per cent, but close enough."

"So, you're telling me that a squad of soldiers landed near your outpost, carrying a spore from a deadly planet-killer, that isn't even found in this arm of the galaxy, and opened it up right in front of you." Litton peered over the top of his glasses in a way that suggested he wasn't convinced.

Aecola's violet eyes welled up as the magnitude of the claim threatened to overwhelm her. It was inconceivable, yet she knew what she had seen. She pulled her datapad from her pack and accessed the recording, handing it over to Litton. He watched it with pursed lips and a furrowed brow, Caden leaning in over his shoulder. When it ended, he handed it back to Aecola.

"Okay," he said. "Granted, we have a squad of soldiers opening something that looks like a fungal spore, while wearing hazmat suits. And, clearly, you've not spent the last three months sat in your outpost faking this." Aecola started to protest but Litton just held up a hand. "I'm not saying I thought you had, I'm just discounting the alternatives out loud. Now, obviously, whatever it is, it isn't good. That's evident by the way they're handling it. But Eschatonus?"

Aecola slumped a little in her seat. The three were back at Caden and Litton's outpost, drinking a brew from Litton's homeworld that Aecola didn't recognise. It had a faintly unpleasant tang, but Litton swore by its calming and restorative properties.

The set-up was identical to her own tree house. High in the canopy, accessed by rope, an observation platform that encircled a tree house, in which were two cots, two chairs, a table, minimal cooking facilities and a flight case containing their personal property. It was, it had to be said, not as tidy as Bokka and Aecola had kept theirs. Bachelor students were the same the galaxy over, it seemed. Still, the familiarity was comforting.

"Even if it's not an Eschatonus spore, if they're taking that much care around it, it must be dangerous. It's clearly dodgy as hell, this is worrying," said Caden.

"I'm not disagreeing with that. I'm just trying to cover all the angles. Maybe it's something that's toxic to humans but is a benevolent part of the Netaran ecosystem. It could be an anti-logging measure, to keep people out. Or an officially sanctioned experimental release of some kind. There are programmes all over Netaris to help with crop parasites. Could that be it?"

"Bokka didn't recognise it, I'm sure. And you think if it was above board, they'd have shot at us? They killed Bokka!"

"We don't know they were shooting to kill."

ESCHATONUS

"They weren't shooting not to," said Aecola, angrily.

"Aecola, Litton can be a little brusque, but he's just trying to work through the situation logically," said Caden, holding out a placating hand. "Litton, a little sensitivity?"

"I'm sorry," said Litton. "Genuinely. Caden's right, I'm a bit too analytical at times. I am sorry about your friend and you're right; this is really messed up. Something dark is obviously going on, I'm just trying to work out what."

Aecola nodded and took another sip of tea.

"So, let's think about what we can say with certainty. We have a secretive operation, which the military are willing to kill to keep under wraps, that involves something they really don't want to come into contact with, that they've just released into the forest."

"That much seems beyond doubt," agreed Caden.

"It would certainly explain the visit we had yesterday."

Aecola looked up, startled.

"They were here?"

"Pretty sure it wasn't these guys," said Litton, gesturing with the datapad. "But it was military. Uniformed military. They said we were here illegally, called in for us to be picked up and confiscated our uplink."

The colour drained from Aecola's face. "You mean you've no way of contacting the university?"

"Not until tomorrow night when our pick-up gets here," said Caden.

"Tomorrow night? Why so long?"

"I don't know. I mean, it's not an emergency evac, maybe it's a question of available fliers." He shared a look with Litton. "We do know we're not the only team being flown out."

"At least four other teams are being withdrawn, all from this region. Ostensibly, we've been told that the government department responsible for the sector has deemed our unli- cenced monitoring programme illegal which, when they said it, didn't surprise us. The fact that they'd be more concerned about us being here than the loggers is about par for the course for this administration. I guess now though we should assume it's because of this operation."

"They didn't fly you out themselves, though, or arrest you."

"Too much noise, I suppose. They wouldn't want the newscasts full of stories about soldiers detaining students, especially non-Netarans, or us asking questions about how quickly we were removed. Much better just to make it look like a standard, routine procedure and let us go back to our studies or start monitoring another sector. And if the operation is that top secret, chances are the grunts on the ground aren't in on it. I'd put money on the guys that were here believing every word they said to us."

"You're just waiting for your pick-up then."

Litton and Caden shared another look. "We were, until we saw a ship come down in the forest a way off to the east."

"That's where we were headed when you jumped out at us," said Caden. "Litton thinks they crashed, although it's impossible to say from this distance. They were coming down fast though."

"Clearly too fast for a controlled landing," said Litton.

"Whatever. Point is, we were going to see what was going on."

Aecola looked from one to the other. "Shall we then?"

The going became easier once they finally stumbled out of the forest into the gaping scar left by the ship's passage through the trees. The ship had cleaved an immense track through the forest, first taking out branches, then whole trees before finally digging into the earth itself. Ground that hadn't seen full daylight in decades was now raw and exposed. Carrion birds were already scouring the site, pulling at bits of crushed animal corpses.

Caden swore softly. "Well, you were right, Litton, this was no controlled landing."

"You think?" Litton's tone was brusque. He wiped at his face with the front of his shirt, his prematurely thinning hair slicked down with sweat. Litton was not built for hiking.

"Come on," said Aecola, pointing. "Down there."

About half a mile away they could see the rear of the ship where it had finally come to a stop.

"Looks like it's still in one piece," said Caden.

"Only one way to find out," replied Litton, following Aecola as she started off towards the ship.

"Hey guys? Are we sure about this?"

Litton and Aecola turned back to look at Caden, Litton holding out his arms in a questioning gesture.

"I mean," said Caden, nervously, "With everything else going on, do we know what might be down there?"

"If one squad came in on a flier carrying the spore in controlled conditions," replied Litton in a sour tone, "I doubt there was a stage two whereby they crashed a freighter into the forest to finish the job."

"He's right," said Aecola. "Whatever this is, I don't see how it's related to what I saw. And you said it yourself, the crew might be wounded and in need of help. Now you want to hold back?"

"I just think... Let's just be careful, okay?"

Aecola nodded. "Okay. Caution's the word of the day, let's go."

The three walked down the trail of destruction towards the ship and then, as they got close, they skirted around and approached from within the trees, alert to any signs of the military.

Aecola was leading and as they drew level with the ship, she waved the others down. As she crouched behind a fallen tree, Caden and Litton crept up either side of her, as quietly as they could.

Two people stood beside the ship, tending to a headwound on a third, seated figure. The injured man was conscious and sitting upright, although the people helping him were showing obvious signs of concern as they dressed the wound.

"They don't look like military," whispered Caden.

"Well, if they are, that's one crappy army," replied Litton.

Aecola, straining to overhear any conversation, flashed him a look, to which Litton raised his hands in apology.

Caden was right, though, the three strangers certainly didn't look in any way military. The woman had striking blue hair, tied into a series of plaits collected up in a band. She wore a light blue jumpsuit, with a staff strapped to her back, and looked trim and athletic. The seated figure with the headwound was dressed in non-descript trousers and boots and a battered old flight jacket. Good looking, Aecola thought, or at least he might be if it wasn't for the ratty moustache and the woeful travesty of a haircut. He looked like every deadbeat pilot back home, she realised, and was no doubt responsible for the ship's crash landing. The third figure had their back to where the activists were concealed, but was tall, dressed all in black, with straggly, sandy coloured hair. When Aecola did catch a glimpse of their face, the bottom half was hidden behind a scarf pulled up over their nose. The eyes, though... Aecola involuntarily ducked back as the figure glanced around at the trees, the eyes appearing to see everything. Aecola held her breath.

The blue-haired woman helped the pilot to his feet. After a moment he seemed to signal that he was okay, so she let him stand unaided. At that point he turned around, slowly, to look at his ship.

"Come on," said Aecola. "They're clearly not military, let's see if they need anything."

"Wait," said Caden. "They're also clearly not seriously injured. Do we want to draw attention to ourselves?"

"You can tell there's nobody else inside the ship, then?" asked Litton, getting to his feet.

At the sound of Litton standing, the three people from the ship spun around. Litton stepped out from the trees, followed by Aecola and a reluctant Caden. Litton held his hands up.

"Hey there. You look like you could do with some help."

VI

The movement startled them, making them spin around. Lukasz reached out a hand as he turned, the swiftness with which he moved making him dizzy for a moment. Xin took his hand and steadied him.

"Hey there, you look like you could do with some help."

"Hello! Yeah, we took a bit of a tumble coming in," called back Wiktoria. "Test flight."

"Looks like it failed," replied the man, smiling. He lowered his arms and started to walk towards them. He looked like he'd been hiking for miles, judging by the sweat patches on his shirt. As he got closer, Wiktoria realised he was younger than he looked from a distance, the thinning hair a bit of a red herring. He actually looked as if he was younger than them. Behind him came an attractive, dark-skinned girl and another man. The second man was bigger, broader across the shoulders than the first, and had a thick moustache that made him, too, look older than he was. Despite being the largest, more capable looking of the three, he also looked the most anxious.

"You could say that," agreed Wiktoria. "I'm Wiktoria, this is Lukasz and Xin."

"Litton," said the young man, holding out his hand, which Wiktoria grasped and shook. "That's Aecola and Caden."

Hands were shaken, other than Xin, who bowed their head at the newcomers, but declined to touch anyone.

"You're all okay? There any more of you?" asked Aecola.

"Took a bump, but I'm okay, I think," said Lukasz. "And no,

this is us."

"You from Netaris?" asked Caden.

"Netaris?" Lukasz turned and fixed Xin with a hard stare. Xin just shrugged.

"Um, no," said Wiktoria. "Tethree. We were heading for Traikker."

"Traikker?" repeated Aecola. "You're some way off course."

"Yeah, it seems like we are. Netaris," repeated Lukasz to himself in disbelief.

Litton started to look over the ship. "She looks old. Held up well though."

"Kept us alive," said Wiktoria, gratefully. "Given the patching up we had to do on the hull, I'm frankly amazed she's still in one piece."

"Clearly you did a good job," replied Litton.

"Not so much on the internal systems, obviously," said Lukasz.

Xin started tapping their fingers.

"It's okay," said Lukasz, waving a hand wearily. "It's an old ship and we were testing her. That's what tests are for, because you don't know if something's right yet. We're alive, we're in one piece, let's not sweat it." He clapped Xin gently on the shoulder. "Let's get in there and see what we do now."

"Want a hand? I did a little engineering back home," offered Litton.

"Good idea," said Aecola. "We could do with some food and a rest before we head back anyway, and I dare say you guys could do with something to eat too." She pulled off her backpack and started rummaging. "Let's sort out some food, you can see what shape the ship's in and then you can decide what you need to do next. First though, can we use your comms?"

"Just our luck."

Aecola stepped back quickly as Lukasz swept past her, his face as black as thunder. Her heart sank as the small hope that she could upload the recording and her troubles might be over shrank and disappeared.

The comms were out, as was the rest of the flight console. The ship still had some power, but it wasn't going anywhere soon. Lukasz kicked a few doors on his way down to where Wiktoria was checking over the engines.

"Any joy?"

"A few hours' work and she'll be running like a dream. And nothing I can't do in situ. No problem," she said, replacing a maintenance panel. Then she saw his expression. "I take it that's not the story up there."

"Can't get a flicker out of the cockpit. No comms, nothing."

"Could be something as simple as tracing a broken connection."

Lukasz sat down and ran a hand over his face.

"Yeah, I guess. I've got Xin on it now."

"Speaking of, don't be too hard on them, yeah? It's an insanely complex bit of kit."

Lukasz waved his hand. "We don't even know that that was where the issue was. Heap of junk like this, anything might have blown anywhere and thrown the whole electrics out. Of course I'm not blaming them."

"Well, tell them that, yeah?"

Lukasz took a deep breath and let it out slowly. "Will do."

"And our guests?"

"What about them?"

"You think they could help us out?"

"Depends on what we need done. If it's a case of getting parts from somewhere, hopefully they can point us in the right direction. They seem friendly enough. That Litton kid's a little strange, but sure, they seem okay."

Wiktoria grinned. "Let's go see what they've sorted out for lunch then."

They ate outside the ship. It was a nice day and as Aecola pointed out, it wasn't often they got to sit out in full sunshine here in the forest. Besides, there was a smell of burnt-out circuitry pervading the ship, on top of the mustiness that still lingered from decades of abandonment.

Caden, being the only one of the six with no practical knowledge to offer on the ship's repairs, had thrown together a meal from what the activists had brought in their packs and some of the supplies on the *Farewell to Tethree*. Some of the ship's ration packs were self-heating, which meant a more exotic meal than the activists had seen in months. The prospect of that seemed to have quelled any doubts Caden may have had about the strangers.

The six sat in a rough circle and ate. Xin sat turned slightly away from the circle, as the necessity of lowering their scarf in front of people made them anxious. As the group ate, they chatted. Lukasz gave the students a quick outline of how he'd become a ship's captain; and Aecola and Litton told the crew some of what they were doing out here in the forest.

"So, wait, they just took your uplink and left you out here?"

"They let us contact the university before they took it, to arrange a pick-up."

"How do they know you weren't the ones who saw the guys with the fungus?"

"Too far away, maybe?" suggested Caden. "That and there's two of us. If they know we operate in pairs, which they almost certainly do by now, they're looking for someone on their own."

"And that's if they haven't managed to identify me specifically," said Aecola, her voice tinged with fear.

"Besides, they were regular military," said Litton. "I doubt anyone told them why we were being cleared out. Anyway, they supervised the call to the university. We're being flown back to Talos tomorrow night."

Lukasz looked up from his bowl. "You think they'd have room for one of us? If we do need any parts, which we should know in a couple of hours, then if you could get one of us to the city, it would be an enormous help."

"Sure," said Caden, "I don't see why not."

"I was thinking," said Litton, "if it would help, we could stay here tonight. You'll need us to wait while you draw up your shopping list, by which time it'll be a bit late to be starting back anyway. We could help out with some of the repairs, bed down in the ship for the night, then all head back to the outpost tomorrow. We'd still be back in plenty of time for the pick-up."

Lukasz and Wiktoria exchanged a look. "I don't see why not," the pilot said. "Makes sense."

"Done."

Lukasz came down the cargo ramp to where the others were taking a break, Xin close behind him, and dropped a pair of charred, blackened power couplings on the ground. Wiktoria passed him up a water bottle, which he drank from before pouring some out on his hands in a pointless attempt at cleaning them. The sun was just setting below the trees and the temperature was starting to drop.

"What's the verdict then?" asked Wiktoria.

Lukasz shook his head. "It's a no-go. We've got no way of getting power back to the flight deck without replacing those. They're totally shot."

"Can't you take them from one of the non-critical systems, just to get you back in the air so you can fly to Talos?" asked Aecola.

"What non-critical systems?" asked Lukasz, bitterly. He then relented, "Sorry, I'm just frazzled. Truth is there are a handful of non-critical systems, but only a handful. This bucket is old, looks like she was flying on just the basics by the end. And what non-critical systems there are, have been repaired so many times that virtually nothing on the ship is standardised. The couplings used on the flight deck are virtually unique, there's nowhere to take any replacements *from*. If the ship still had its shuttle, we might be able to use that but, of course, it doesn't."

"So, Plan B," said Litton. "You come back to the outpost with us tomorrow, hitch a ride back to Talos, buy what you need and then get someone to fly you out here again."

"If they have the parts we need," said Wiktoria. "She's pretty much obsolete."

Lukasz shook his head. "Not an issue. We'll just get a whole new power array. We need to start standardising anyway and we should have enough cash to score a basic set-up. Just. I don't want to go through this every time something blows. Which I have a nasty feeling is going to be quite often."

"That's settled then," said Caden.

Lukasz flopped down on the ground next to Wiktoria, who gave him a reassuring pat on the head. "I guess so. Thank you, guys. This would have taken a lot longer without you."

"Not to mention the fact we'd have been stuck out here without even a clue which way the nearest town was. We got lucky, Lukasz. I think maybe we should have thought this out a bit more first in terms of emergency preparation."

"Easy to say after the event," said Litton. "Don't beat yourselves up. We did find you; we can get you to civilisation, no harm done. Now, who's up for a little drink." He pulled a bottle out of his pack, a sly smile on his face.

"Oh man, is that what I think it is?" asked Caden. "I thought we'd finished it all weeks ago."

"Always keep some back, Cade, just in case." Litton winked at him.

Lukasz woke up with a sore head. Not as sore as the crew, he'd wager. Wiktoria hadn't let him drink last night, on account of the bang to the head he'd taken in the crash. Judging by the noise they were still making after he turned in, he'd be lucky if anyone else was ready to go anywhere before midday. He pulled his trousers and boots on and stepped out of his cabin. The rest of the ship was silent, save for a low rumbling from a cabin that, Lukasz guessed, held Caden and Litton. It wasn't the one Wiktoria had chosen and Xin was sleeping in the nest. Surely Aecola didn't snore like that?

He grinned to himself and headed down to the galley to boil some water for a brew then, when he'd made himself a steaming mug of coffee, he made his way down to the cargo hold and hit the controls on the ramp.

Sunlight streamed in as the ramp lowered and Lukasz shielded his eyes as he stepped outside. It looked like it was going to be another glorious day. Good job too, if they were going to be hiking for much of it. He stood for a moment, enjoying the feel of the sun on his bare chest. Then he heard a noise behind him. Turning, he saw Aecola descending from the gantry into the hold, still in the vest-top and shorts she'd slept in. He realised he was staring at her legs as she made her way down the ladder and quickly looked away, taking another mouthful of coffee. She waved at him as she came out to join him.

"You don't look like someone who was up drinking all night." She gave him a warm smile and patted him on the arm.

"Don't be bitter, grandad, just because I'm still young enough to brush a night like that off before breakfast. If I was back at the university, I'd already be planning where to go out tonight."

"Grandad," scoffed Lukasz. "I'm all of, what, five years older than you?"

"And the rest," she joked. "Anyone else up yet?" She looked up at him, her violet eyes sparkling.

"No sign of Wiktoria or your friends. Xin was doing something with the navi-computer when I came past."

"I'll go get them up, get us some breakfast. Then we ought to make a move."

"I guess so," said Lukasz, taking a last swig from his mug before emptying the dregs on the ground.

A light breakfast was all anyone was in the mood for, so it wasn't long before the six were stood outside, the others watching while Lukasz raised the cargo ramp and secured the ship. Then with a final check on his datapad for their current position, Lukasz followed Wiktoria, Xin and the students into the woods.

They made good time and, despite Wiktoria being a little tetchy from the late night, the mood was good. They chatted freely as they hiked, Xin sticking close to Wiktoria, occasionally signing something at her that she shared with the group. A few hours passed and they were approaching the outpost when Caden, who was leading at that point, held up a hand.

"What...?" started Litton, but was shushed by Caden frantically waving his hand, still looking ahead. Then he turned to face them, a finger to his lips.

Lukasz stepped up to where Caden was stood and whispered, "What is it?"

"I'm sure I heard voices ahead."

"The pick-up?"

"They're early if it is." Caden checked his watch. "They're not due for another couple of hours."

"Tell the rest to wait here, we'll check it out."

Caden took a few paces back to Aecola and told her to get the others to wait, then he and Lukasz made their way carefully forward.

Ahead of them, they could make out a group of men, one talking and gesturing at the others.

"You recognise them?"

"No, but they're armed."

"Military then?"

"I guess so."

"Are we near your camp?"

"Near it? They're stood right under it."

Sure enough, Lukasz could now see the ropes hanging down from the tree near where the men were stood. As Caden had said, they were armed. There were five men, four of them with pulse rifles, all listening to the fifth as he, presumably, issued his instructions. They weren't in uniform, just non-descript camouflaged gear.

"This doesn't look good."

"Too right, it doesn't," whispered Aecola, making the two men jump.

"For crying out loud," said Caden, as loudly as he dared. "You scared the hell out of us."

Aecola ignored him, pointing at the men by the outpost. "They're the same soldiers I saw with the Eschatonus."

VII

"No-one up top, sir," reported Zane, the last soldier to shimmy down the rope. He unslung his pulse rifle as he hit the ground, ready for action.

Petru stood with his hands on his hips, looking around as if willing Aecola to appear. "Dammit. And you're sure they haven't been picked up already?"

Jekk was carrying a military-grade uplink in his gear, which he currently had wired to his datapad. "So far as we know, their pick-up is scheduled for two hours from now. We're tracking the university flier; it seems to be sticking to its flight plan. There was a ship came down yesterday in the region..."

Petru spun around to face him. "What? Why didn't you tell me that?"

"It came from out of system. Military deemed it insignificant, passed it on to civilian air control, who only just logged it," shrugged Jekk. "Came out of hollow space far too close to the planet, promptly lost control and went down. The location of the crash site's unknown, I only mention it because it's likely to be in this sector. But if it was a rendezvous, doesn't look like a successful one. And there's no trace of these activists being funded from out of system in any case. I don't see that it's anything to do with..."

"So it has nothing to do with them. Doesn't mean they didn't see it come down and went to investigate, does it," snapped Petru.

"No sir," said Jekk, chafing somewhat at the reprimand and

the fact he could see Tyger and Zane smirking at him from behind Petru.

"What do we do now, sir?" asked Goff.

Petru thought for a moment, again eyeing the forest as he did so. "If they went out yesterday to check the crash out," he said quietly, almost to himself, "and they know their pick-up is due…"

"They're moving out!"

Aecola breathed a sigh of relief and slumped against the tree she was hiding behind. For a moment there, it looked as if her one chance of getting out of here had just evaporated.

"That's odd," said Litton. The other three had crept up to where Caden, Lukasz and Aecola were concealed and all six watched as the soldiers moved off, heading away from them.

"What?"

"They must be aware of your crash. Surely they'd be heading in this direction to check it out."

"Let's just be thankful that they aren't," replied Aecola, getting to her feet and adjusting her pack.

"Hang on," said Wiktoria, grabbing Aecola's wrist. "Let them get a good distance away. It's not like we haven't the time."

They waited for twenty anxious minutes before Lukasz said, "Right, that ought to do it. Let's go."

They got up and slowly made their way to the outpost. Hesitantly, Litton was the first to step out into the slightly clearer area around their tree. He walked over to the rope system that they had watched the soldiers descend a short while before, trying to act as if he'd no idea the outpost had recently had visitors. The others tentatively followed, all except Aecola, who stayed hidden in the bushes.

Nothing happened.

They paused, looking around as if they expected the soldiers to swoop out at any moment, but the forest was quiet. "I think we're good," said Litton. He reached out, grabbed the saddle slung at the bottom of the ropes and climbed in. "I'll go up, Caden can follow, and we'll start ferrying our belongings down ready for the pick-up."

With that, he started pulling on one of the other ropes,

winching himself skywards.

It took about an hour for Caden and Litton to sort out their belongings, pack and lower the gear to the forest floor. There was a small disagreement about whether they should be bringing all the Enviro-subcommittee's equipment as well but, in the end, Litton argued that as they weren't being replaced and were unlikely to be back anytime soon, the equipment ought to be coming back with them. They brought down as much as they could carry, but it proved beyond any of them to work out how to disassemble the rope system from the ground, so in the end they had to leave it rigged up.

"If we'd had a chance to talk properly to them, we could have gotten some instructions for it," griped Caden.

"Frankly, that's the least of our worries," replied Litton. "Russell can come and dismantle his own damned rigging. Tonight, I'm sleeping in my own bed back at the dorm, away from soldiers with guns, and that's the last I want to think about any of this. No offence, Aec."

"None taken, that's all I'm thinking too."

The clearing that served as a landing site for the university flier was only a few minutes from the outpost, so the group took up the small pile of crates and bags and headed over to it. There, they dumped the gear in a heap and sat down, waiting for the flier.

Litton and Caden pulled out their datapads, linking the two to play a strategy game to pass the time, Xin watching over Caden's shoulder. Wiktoria gently unwrapped the dressing on Lukasz's head to give his bump another check. Aecola was still nervous, looking around at the surrounding trees. She didn't let herself think of herself as home and dry. *Not until I'm on the flier and we've taken off.* She anxiously checked her watch. "What time are they supposed to be here?"

Litton, his eyes still locked on his screen, opened his mouth to answer, then paused and held up a finger. Seconds later, they all heard it, the distant but unmistakable hum of an incoming flier. He grinned at Aecola, who gave him a tense smile in return.

A few minutes later, the flier appeared over the trees and applied its airbrakes, turning slightly as it prepared to land. The activists and Lukasz's crew stood up, stretching their limbs, and starting to pick up bits and pieces from the heaped pile of Litton and Caden's gear.

None of them saw the rocket trail from the trees the far side of the clearing, so nobody had a clue what was happening when the flier exploded, showering the clearing with debris, and filling the air with the smell of burning fuel. The six instinctively threw themselves on the ground, yelling at each other and all trying to work out at once if they were all okay. Flaming parts of the wrecked flier were dropping to the ground around them, to the sound of smaller, secondary explosions.

"Quiet! Everybody calm dow…"

Caden was the first to his feet, looking around the clearing, through the smoke, searching for Litton. He never saw the man that shot him, there was no time for him to register the attack before the blast from the pulse rifle caught him in the back of the head, killing him instantly. His body crumpled, toppling over, and falling right next to Aecola, his mangled face staring at her from his dead eyes.

She screamed.

"Lukasz! Lukasz!" Someone was shaking him, he registered, his head fuzzy and his ears ringing. Was it time to get up? Where was he?

He put a hand to his throbbing forehead. It felt damp. Looking in bewilderment at his fingers, he saw blood. What the hell?

"Lukasz, come on, we've got to move!" the voice said, urgently. He started to sit up, then a wave of dizziness came over him and he threw up. He slumped down again, but the person who'd woken him yanked his arm and he stumbled to his feet.

"Wiktoria? What…?"

The air was filled with smoke and the smell of burning. Visibility was extremely limited. He wondered where he was as he looked at the ground around his feet.

"The flier's been shot down! We have to go!" Wiktoria's voice was highly agitated, urgent.

Over the ringing of his ears, he realised he could hear the buzz of multiple pulse rifles. The noise sharpened his senses and adrenalin started to kick in. With Wiktoria's help, he started to stumble for the treeline. Luckily the smoke from the crash was making it hard for whoever was shooting at them to pick out their targets and they seemed to be just firing blindly into the chaos in hope.

"Where's Xin?"

"I don't know," she started to say. At the same time, Xin appeared at the treeline, waving to them, urging them on. They were almost there when someone appeared from out of the forest behind Xin.

"Look out!" yelled Wiktoria.

Xin dropped instinctively to one knee and spun around. The man, expecting to take Xin by surprise, almost tripped over them and was caught off guard by the fist suddenly slammed into his stomach. Winded, the man tried to bring his rifle to bear on Xin but by this time Wiktoria, still running towards the pair, had pulled the staff from her back and she lunged at the soldier, catching him in the throat with the tip of her weapon. He fell choking to his knees and Lukasz, now right behind Wiktoria, made a grab for the pulse rifle. He swung it around, catching the man on the temple with the butt of the gun and knocking him out cold.

"What the hell is going on?"

"They must have known about the evac," said Aecola, staggering out from the smoke on their left, her face smudged and tearful. "We have to get out of here."

"What about Litton?" said Wiktoria. "And Caden?"

"Caden's dead," said Aecola, bitterly.

The four plunged into the undergrowth, trying to put distance between themselves and the attacking soldiers. They made it about thirty feet before Lukasz grabbed Aecola and pulled her down to the ground, Wiktoria and Xin following suit. Another soldier had appeared, over to their right, running towards the clearing. The four, panting heavily, froze in terror, but the man hadn't seen them and just kept running, his rifle held out before him.

Lukasz waited until the man was almost at the edge of the trees, now with his back to them, then raised his own rifle and fired. The soldier crumpled as the pulse from Lukasz's rifle caught him in the back.

"Move!" urged Lukasz, pulling Aecola up by the arm and running further into the forest.

They didn't see anyone else as they fled and, after a few minutes, they dropped to their knees again behind a fallen tree that rested at the edge of a shallow depression. Aecola and Wiktoria ducked down completely, while Lukasz knelt, leaning against the fallen tree trunk, his stolen rifle facing back in the direction they had run, anxiously sweeping the barrel in a wide arc as he desperately looked for any signs of pursuit.

Xin calmly put their hand on the barrel, holding the gun still. "They'll see the movement," they whispered.

Lukasz, still gulping in air, nodded and forced himself to relax, steadying his rifle but keeping a sharp lookout.

"You're wounded," whispered Xin, gently taking the pulse rifle from Lukasz and assuming his position.

Lukasz let himself slide to the floor with his back to the trunk. He put his hand to his head again and winced as he located the wound.

"Here," said Wiktoria, "let me." She had been putting her pack on again when the flier exploded, so fortunately still had the kit she'd brought from the ship, including a small first aid pack. She cleansed the wound, then applied a dressing. "I don't think it's deep. Head wounds always look bad, they tend to be bleeders."

They were silent for a moment, the sound of the burning flier starting to fade to the point where they could now hear voices calling to each other over the top of the crackling flames.

"I'm sorry I got you caught up in all this," said Aecola, miserably.

"Well, we're going to need you to help us out of it, as we don't have a clue where we are and we're obviously not getting a ride out of here any time soon," replied Lukasz, his tone level as he tried not to show his anger and frustration. Wiktoria glanced at him, in a way that suggested he hadn't been entirely successful in hiding it.

Aecola wiped at her eyes, nodding.

Xin put their hand down and shook Lukasz's shoulder, prompting the pilot to sit up and look where Xin was indicating. Staggering towards them, cradling one arm, was Litton, his face a picture of pain and terror.

"Soldiers... coming..." the activist started.

Lukasz stood up and took the rifle back from Xin, who seemed more than content to hand it over. "Xin, help Litton. Wiktoria and Aecola, lead us away from here, any direction, as quick as you like. I'll wait for five minutes, then follow you."

There were still no signs of pursuit by the time Lukasz slipped away to follow the others. His best guess was that the soldiers had regrouped to decide on their next course of action. Finding the two men they'd taken out and checking the wreckage would have taken a certain amount of time. If the soldier Wiktoria had struck in the throat had needed medical attention, that too might have bought them a little time, depending on how big the squad was. That was a whole lot of guesses and assumptions, though. Lukasz was torn. They hadn't asked to get pulled into whatever this shitshow was, but it was also true that they could have landed miles away from anyone and been unable to even begin trying to get help. All this aside, they were probably still luckier than not that they'd been found by Aecola and the others. So long as they could get out of here without getting killed.

Jogging, he soon caught the rest up, shaking his head to Wiktoria's unspoken question. The five of them marched on, Wiktoria leading and trying not to create too much of a trail, Lukasz bringing up the rear and doing his best to mask what signs they were leaving.

By evening, they were exhausted. Litton was virtually on his knees. He had stubbornly refused to let Wiktoria even look at his hand, shaking his head violently and pulling away every time she suggested it. Eventually, she called a halt to the march. "We need to rest. If they find us, they find us, but we'll still have a better chance if we're rested than if they catch us up while we're stumbling in the dark."

Lukasz reluctantly agreed and they found a hollow to rest in. Wiktoria and Xin were the only ones who had managed to get away with their packs, so it was a dismal meal they put together, a handful of emergency rations each. Shelter was going to be a problem too.

"We need to circle back to the ship and get some more supplies," said Lukasz.

"They'll probably have found it, we'd be walking right into their arms," argued Aecola.

"Maybe not. If their mission is as secret as you say, then we could well be looking at just this squad of five men…"

"Four now, maybe three," corrected Wiktoria.

"… because they're not going to want backup. The fact they had to get other soldiers involved to disband the observation groups would be more involvement than they'd ideally want. We might even outnumber them, if not outgun them," continued Lukasz, looking down with a grim expression at their one pulse rifle. "They'll have checked the ship, but they won't have men to spare guarding it. They'll see it's abandoned and move on. They don't even know it was us that was with you at the pick-up. We could have just been more students, for all they know."

"That's a lot of assumptions you're making."

"It's not unreasonable though," said Wiktoria.

"No, and the fact is if we've now got a week-long hike to the nearest town, then that," said Lukasz, pointing at their meagre supplies, "isn't going to get us there. We're riding our luck whatever we do, I'd rather ride it on a full belly."

VIII

Lukasz lowered the rifle. It had been forty-five minutes since he'd carefully made his way up the tree, tearing his trousers and cutting his leg in the process, and nestled himself into a position from where he could see the ship and the surrounding ground. The scope on the rifle was impressively (and therefore worryingly) high spec and his view was unimpeded. In all that time, there hadn't been the slightest indication that the ship was being guarded. In the end, the appearance of a deer, nosing around the enormous rut from the ship's controlled crash, had settled the question. There was nobody down there.

He shimmied down the trunk again, dropping the last ten feet and slightly winding himself in the process. Still with the utmost caution, he made his way back to where the rest of the group were waiting.

"Not a whisper," he reported.

The sense of relief around the circle was muted, but palpable. Wiktoria gave him a brief smile, before pointedly looking over at Litton again. Lukasz followed her gaze. The activist was getting to be a worry.

Litton had finally let Wiktoria examine him as they rested the night before. His hand was in a hell of a state, charred and broken from where a lump of the wreckage from the flier had hit him, his fingers all but useless. Throwing his arms up was probably the only thing that had saved his life, but it looked like it had nearly cost him his hand. It was the sort of thing a modern medical facility would probably be able to repair reasonably straightforwardly, provided they could get him to one. Out here though, and on the run, shock and infection were a real danger and there was no doubt Litton needed attention just as soon as they could get it. The trouble was, that was at least six days away, even if everything was plain sailing. Which Lukasz doubted it would be.

There was still no sign of pursuit, but Lukasz was sure it was only a matter of time before the soldiers picked up their trail and once that happened, they were bound to start overhauling them. But there was little to be done about that. First things first.

Lukasz led the group to the ship, where he lowered the ramp and paused as they entered, still watching the trees. He waited until they were well inside before walking up the ramp himself, closing it behind him.

Litton was being helped up to the gantry by Wiktoria, watched anxiously by Aecola. Lukasz just caught sight of Xin's back, as they headed to the nest. He followed them in.

"What do you think?" he asked, when the two of them were in Xin's lair.

Xin looked at him and started moving their fingers, signing their concerns.

"You're right, you're right. I've been thinking the same thing. I'd be a whole lot happier if we could just walk away from this. But we would have been lost without them. This Gran Palomos isn't even on our maps, I've checked. On our own, the nearest settlement we'd have been aware of would be weeks away. And besides, we're in it now. It's not like we can leave Litton, not in the state his hand's in."

Xin shrugged, signing a response that made Lukasz raise his eyebrows.

"Yeah, you may be right. Gotta try though. He might make it. Okay, I'm going to go check on them."

He turned to leave, then looked back at Xin. "How am I doing?"

Xin nodded, holding out a hand and giving it a so-so tilt.

"That good?"

Lukasz chuckled and left.

Litton's hand was a real mess. Watched over nervously by Aecola, Wiktoria was doing the best she could to clean the wound, which was at least slightly easier in a partially equipped, basic med-room than it was out in the field. However, it was clear, even to her, that there was an urgent need for proper attention.

"I've done the best I can cleaning it and these dressings are a bit more all-purpose. That should see you right until we get to a doctor," she said, sounding more confident than she felt. "Thank goodness for Erkon," she added to herself.

Litton nodded, "Thank you." He at least looked a better colour now that she had got some generic antibiotics into him and he was sitting down in the warmth.

Lukasz appeared at the door. "How are we looking?"

"We'll manage," said Wiktoria. "I think we need to rest here for the night though, move on tomorrow."

"Aecola?"

"I don't like it, but Wiktoria's right. It's a long hike to Gran Palomos, a decent night's sleep would be a great way to start."

"Okay then, we'll rest up and get going early in the morning."

"I think I should stay here," said Litton.

Wiktoria's expression registered unease at the idea. She looked up at Lukasz, who wordlessly acknowledged her concern.

"I'm worried if this gets any worse and I start struggling, I'm going to slow you up," continued Litton.

"You don't think you'd be better seeing a doctor as soon as possible?" asked Lukasz.

"Absolutely. And when you get to Gran Palomos, you can get a flier and be back here within a few hours. You'll already have saved that time on the hike, and more, by not taking me with you. All things being equal, I'll see a doctor sooner by staying here than I would by going with you."

Lukasz weighed that up for a moment. "You may be right. Let's sleep on it, see how you're doing in the morning."

He turned and left the sickbay, heading for the cargo bay. Wiktoria followed.

"It's not just his hand. I'm worried about his state of mind. It's not like we know him but, even so, he doesn't seem himself to me. And if we leave him here and it gets any worse, or he starts getting an infection, we won't even know about it."

"And if either of those things happen halfway to Gran Palomos, what do we do with him in the woods? He's right, at that point he's only slowing us down, which increases the wait for him to be seen to properly, far more than if the four of us leave him here and make good time."

"Maybe one of us should stay here with him, to keep an eye on him?"

"Nothing doing. Aecola needs to stay on the move, and I need you and Xin with me to make sure we get the parts we need. Not to mention if we run into those soldiers again, we'll need the manpower. If he stays here, he can keep himself dosed up and the wound clean. If he dies here, he would have died in the woods anyway and we'd be sitting ducks. You need to make sure he's got access to what he needs, and not to anything he shouldn't. I know it sounds harsh, but Litton said it himself, it's the best chance he's got at getting that hand seen to quickly. I'm going to go through Erkon's crates, see if he gave us anything more useful than beer." He paused for a moment at the doorway through to the hold's upper gantry. "Send Aecola down, she can help me make up some packs."

"Yes, Captain," said Wiktoria.

"And keep calling me that, I like it."

"Shut up, Lukasz."

Aecola, Xin, Wiktoria and Lukasz sat in the galley around the table. Litton was asleep in the cabin Lukasz had assigned him. The four were sharing a stew that Xin had knocked up from some of the fresh provisions that Erkon had provided, conscious that this was the last decent meal they'd be getting for a few days. They'd also opened a bottle of Tethrian brandy they'd found at the bottom of one of the crates.

"So, you're a monk, not a nun?" Aecola was confused.

"Technically, I'm a sister of the Cavellite Order, but you're correct, I'm not a nun. There are communities of Cavellite nuns on Tethree, but I was raised in a Cavellite monastery, not a convent."

"It's a weirdo sect," chipped in Lukasz. "Tethree is one of the few systems in this sector that you'll find Cavellites. They tend to avoid more populated planets, presumably because of their unorthodox views on traditional gender roles."

"We're not a 'weirdo sect', we're just a minority offshoot of the more traditional Hulaic mainstream theology," sighed Wiktoria, used to Lukasz's baiting. "And our views aren't unorthodox, they're more... well, okay, maybe they are unorthodox. But it's not any kind of schism, we're just a frontier order. Like Lukasz says, our communities tend to settle on out-of-the-way planets, recently terraformed planetoids and newbuild habitats. The places we live, decisions tend to be made by practical demand, not rigid dogma. I was orphaned as a baby and the nearest community to me was a monastery, not a convent, so I was raised by monks."

"Hence why she's so handy with that," said Lukasz, pointing at her staff.

"We do practice our own martial arts. Again, comes with the types of planets we tend to settle on, we like to be able to defend ourselves." Wiktoria knocked back her drink and poured herself another.

"Are you a Cavellite as well?" asked Aecola, looking at Xin, who shook their head.

"Xin is a tech wizard, but very much their own person. Not one for being part of any community, are you, Xin."

Xin gesticulated, a complex string of finger gestures that left Aecola baffled.

"You get used to them," said Wiktoria. "Xin was thrown out by their parents as a teenager, had to make their own way in the world. They fell in with Lukasz, helping out at his yard with the more complicated tech stuff."

Lukasz and Wiktoria fell silent for a moment, remembering what had brought the yard into his possession. Then Xin held up their glass. Lukasz raised his and clinked it against Xin's. "Here's to you, old man," said Lukasz, quietly.

The galley grew quiet. After a moment, Wiktoria leaned back in her chair and yawned. "I guess if we're getting this early start tomorrow..."

"Good idea," said Aecola.

"Come on, let's leave these two to it."

The two girls got up and left, while Lukasz poured himself and Xin another glass of brandy.

There was a light mist over the crash site the next morning when Lukasz let down the ramp and cautiously stepped out. A flock of roosting birds had taken off, startled by the noise of the descending ramp, and he watched as they circled and then came down into the trees again. It was quiet; the reverential, almost prayer-like quiet of the early morning. Deer had gathered a way off from the ship, grazing on the exposed ground. One of them raised its head, chewing as it looked at Lukasz, assessing how much of a threat he posed. Not much of one, clearly, he mused, as it lowered its head again and continued rooting around.

He gave the surrounding area a subtle scan while trying not to make it obvious that that was what he was doing. With an ostentatious yawn, he walked once around the outside of the ship, making out as if he were just checking the hull. If they were being watched, there was every chance that none of the soldiers hunting them had seen enough of him or his crew to recognise them, so Lukasz hoped that it was only Aecola they had any firm description of.

When it was apparent that he wasn't going to be shot on sight, he strode around to the cargo ramp and signalled the group inside. Xin led the way, passing the pulse rifle and Lukasz's pack to him as they stepped off the ramp. Wiktoria and Aecola followed, the latter wearing a hooded top and a scarf over her face much like Xin, her hair tied up and tucked in. It wouldn't fool anyone for long but hopefully a casual observer wouldn't recognise her straight away.

Each of them had a backpack, with rations shared equally among them. They had also, at Aecola's suggestion, included some emergency breathing apparatus, part of the ship's standard repair kit. The most direct route to Gran Palomos took them close to the infection site and, without knowing how far it had spread, they were running the risk of encountering the contamination. If Aecola was right about it being Eschatonus, while it wasn't good to get it on the skin, breathing in the spores was as good as a death sentence.

Xin and Aecola also had bolt-pistols strapped to their thighs. Lukasz swore to himself that he was going to buy Erkon a whole case of brandy when they got back to Tethree, having found the weapons stowed at the bottom of one of the big man's crates, along with some basic emergency supplies, such as a set of lightweight blankets that they also took with them. Clearly the Cavellite had shown a bit more foresight about what they were doing than he, Lukasz, had. They had a lot to think about the next time they flew.

It was chilly, but the sun was starting to burn through the haze and the skies were clearing up. It looked like a good day for hiking.

"Right, let's get on with it. Is Litton okay?"

"He seemed a bit better this morning," said Aecola. "A bit brighter, and more colour in his face."

"I've secured the other cabins, clearly labelled the meds in the sickbay and locked away anything he shouldn't be handling," said Wiktoria. "The flight deck is also secure."

"And the nest?"

Xin gave him a thumbs up.

"Where is he now?"

"He's in the galley having his breakfast."

"Right, I guess we're off then," said Lukasz, raising the ramp. "Lead on, Aecola."

The going was good and the four of them settled into a steady pace. They were still without any kind of signal, but Aecola's datapad had enough geographical data already downloaded that with the internal compass, she was confident both of their location and direction. The first day they made good progress and spirits were high. At the end of the second day, they had made it back to her tree house which, after some deliberation, they decided not to sleep in, as it was the one definite location the soldiers had for her and there was no guarantee it wasn't booby-trapped. It was comforting to all of them, though, that they had reached it at roughly the time Aecola thought they should. Clearly, they were on track. They eventually made camp a short distance from the tree house, setting an overnight watch given their proximity to the outpost.

"How are you doing?"

Aecola, taking the first watch, looked up from where she was stood to see Wiktoria bringing her a steaming cup of tea.

"Okay, I guess," she replied quietly, taking the cup from Wiktoria with both hands, warming them even as she blew across the top to take the edge off the tea. "Trying not to fall apart, if I'm honest."

"You're doing a great job," said Wiktoria, putting her hand on the younger woman's shoulder. "It's a hell of a thing you've been through. You should be proud of how you've kept it together."

Aecola gave her a weak smile and sipped at the tea.

"This fungus," began Wiktoria.

"The Eschatonus."

"Yeah. It's that bad?"

Aecola nodded. "I've never seen it in the flesh, probably less than fifty people have. It's not even found in this arm of the galaxy. It was discovered about thirty years ago by a long-range prospecting mission. It's a planet killer. Its spores can survive deep space, we don't know how. But any planet it lands on, if the conditions are even partway palatable, it takes hold and spreads, killing everything, breaking whole ecosystems down, until the planet is... used up."

Wiktoria swore softly under her breath.

"It's okay," continued Aecola. "It's so far out on the other arm, it wouldn't make planetfall naturally in Federation space for generations. But if someone's managed to retrieve some, bring it back here..."

"Why would anyone do that?"

Aecola drank the last of her tea and handed the cup back to Wiktoria. "I keep asking myself the same question. If they just wanted to clear out the local indigenous population, it's a risky and frankly crazy-hard way of going about it. And the panic it would cause..."

Wiktoria frowned as Aecola paused, the colour draining from her face.

"What is it?"

"The panic. That's what it's for."

"I don't follow."

"The Netaran government's getting a lot of pushback on its environmental credentials at the moment. They've already enacted a lot of deregulation on logging and there's a real feeling that even the regular populace is starting to get concerned about the free hand being given to corporations in how they operate. The new president is pushing ahead with stripping even more current legislation away, allowing companies to do what they want in the forests and leaving no protections in place for the ecosystems as they stand..."

"... and an incident like this, where lives are lost because of an invasive species, will strengthen the case for human interference and management..."

"... and so who's going to argue against it?"

IX

The next morning, after another ecological lecture on the potential danger of fungal infection and the signs to look out for, they set off for Gran Palomos.

There was a definite change of atmosphere now. Aecola was a lot warier, keeping her eyes peeled for anything out of the ordinary, and her caution rubbed off on the others. Chat was less and, if anything, their speed increased. The group seemed to reach an unspoken consensus that this part of the journey should be got through as quickly as possible. Lunch on the third day of their hike was a hurried affair, although Lukasz insisted that they still take the same time to rest. Consistency was the key, he argued, and they wouldn't get anywhere quicker by tiring themselves out. By the afternoon, all of them had sensed a subtle shift in the air. There was less birdsong, less activity. Even Lukasz, who had as little affinity with nature as any man alive, could feel that this part of the forest was less populated by the small mammals, insects and birds that made up the ecosystem in this part of Netaris. By early evening, Wiktoria had started to notice a change in the background odour of the forest. Aecola confirmed it.

"Should we be wearing our breathing gear?"

Aecola shook her head. "Not necessary. It's not the smell, it's the spores we need to avoid. The smell is likely to get quite a bit worse before we're in any danger of exposure."

"But we're heading into it?" asked Lukasz.

"Again, not so much. We're actually bypassing the initial infection site by some miles, we're more straying into the zone around the current infection area, at a tangent. This may be as much as we experience before we get past it."

Lukasz kept to himself the thought that she didn't sound as confident of that as she claimed.

They pressed on.

"Lukasz! Lukasz!"

"Wha... whassat?"

Lukasz was being shaken by the arm. He pulled away, irritably, feeling like he could barely remember the last time he was allowed to just wake up naturally on his own damn terms.

"Lukasz, I think we need to wake the others."

It was Aecola. She had taken the last watch, so it couldn't be too long before dawn, according to Lukasz's groggy calculations.

They had bedded down for the night in a natural hollow, the lightweight emergency blankets doing a good job of keeping them warm despite their thinness. Lukasz sat up, rubbing at his neck which was stiff from using his pack as a pillow.

"What is it?" he asked more clearly, trying to swallow down his irritation.

Aecola didn't answer, but instead got to her feet and walked a few yards away from their camp. He followed her to a bush, where she gingerly held one of the branches back and shone a light on it.

"I don't... What am I looking at?"

Aecola moved her torch slightly, the change of angle catching something on the leaves, making a slight glint.

"What is it?"

"Mycelium."

He stared at her blankly and waited for an answer he understood.

"It's the vegetative part of a fungus."

Lukasz nearly tripped over backing away from the bush. "You mean that's...?"

"I don't know," admitted Aecola, "but it's not something I'd normally expect to see above ground, not with any species I'm familiar with. There's plenty of these bushes by the outpost and I've not seen them show any signs of this sort of fungal infection."

Lukasz looked back to where the others were sleeping.

"How did you even…?"

Aecola flushed slightly. "I needed some privacy and so I came over here. I got my torch out so I wouldn't trip on the way back."

"Still, good eyes."

"I've been looking out for it since we left my outpost," she confessed.

"I thought you seemed extra cautious."

Aecola let go of the branch slowly to avoid disturbing the eerie strands. Lukasz took hold of her arm and gently pulled her away from the bush.

"Have you found any more of it?"

"Not as yet. But still, if we're on the fringe of the actual area of contamination, I think I want to get on as quickly as possible."

"We still don't know that it is this Eschat… Eschot…"

"Eschatonus. No, we don't," she agreed, "but whatever it is, the soldiers didn't want to touch it, so I'm damned sure I don't want to, either."

Lukasz nodded and checked his watch. "Okay, we're a couple of hours early but we've been taking it at a steady pace, a longer day to get past this wouldn't hurt. If we move past it, we can stop early if we need to. Breathing apparatus?"

"Not yet. The mycelium might not be able to reproduce yet. It's when we see the fruiting part that we need to start taking care. Gloves wouldn't hurt though."

Lukasz couldn't stop himself looking down. Yes, Aecola was wearing hers.

"Right, let's get the others."

Wiktoria paled when Aecola described what she'd seen. Xin, hair hanging low and their scarf pulled up, didn't show any emotion, but their eyes widened slightly.

"It doesn't mean we're in the danger zone, just getting close," said Lukasz, looking to Aecola for back up. She nodded. "It's a good argument for an early start and a strong pace, though."

"If I'm honest, I'm slightly surprised to find it's spread this far," said Aecola. "It's not my area of expertise, though, and I guess the environment it finds itself in will dictate that to some degree. Elsewise it could have been spread by wildlife. Or not be the Eschatonus at all. I would just rather leave it an unexplained mystery than find out, if I'm honest."

"I'm with you on that," said Wiktoria.

Aecola started off at a brisk pace which Lukasz gave her free rein over until they'd been on their way for about an hour, at which point he slowed them down a bit. "It's a marathon, not a sprint. I want to be out of here as quickly as you do, so let's not burn out, or turn an ankle."

Aecola nodded and modified her pace, all the while keeping as sharp an eye out as she could for any sign of infection in the surrounding plant life, until Lukasz pointedly asked her to keep her focus on their route.

By midday, she had started to relax a little. Although the forest was now eerily quiet, none of them had seen any signs of any untoward growth on any of the trees or bushes they'd passed. When they stopped for lunch, at one point Lukasz nudged Aecola and silently indicated a nearby tree branch with his sandwich. A small rodent was watching them, until it realised it had been spotted and scampered off. A good sign.

Late in the afternoon, but slightly earlier than they had stopped the previous three days, Lukasz pulled them in. "We've made good ground today, but we had an early start, so I think we should rest."

Aecola looked reluctant but of the four of them, she was probably the most tired, so didn't protest. Wiktoria and Xin went off to perform a sweep of the immediate area, while Lukasz and Aecola sat down and looked at the map on her datapad.

"So far as I can make out, we're within a mile or so of here," she said, indicating with the cursor a spot on the map. She zoomed out, showing both the previous points she'd logged marking their progress and Gran Palomos ahead of them. Lukasz didn't mention the small black flag icon she'd logged at the previous night's camp. The reason for it was clear.

"Looking at that, three days?"

"About that. I reckoned about five or six from the tree house, so given our pace, that would fit."

Lukasz let out a small grunt of satisfaction. So far so good. They seemed to be clear of the infected zone and there had been no sign of the soldiers. Three days hiking and there was a warm bath, a hot meal and replacement parts waiting for them. And, if their luck held, a quick flight back to the crash site, Litton and his ship.

"Thank you, Lukasz."

"For what?" He looked up from the datapad.

"Sticking with me," said Aecola, leaning into him slightly, elbowing him softly in the ribs. "Keeping me in check today. Helping me."

He shrugged awkwardly. "Just made sense, is all. And it's not like I could leave you. We could leave you," he corrected himself. This close to her, he realised, he had become very aware of her body and for someone who'd been hiking for the best part of a week, she smelled surprisingly good.

She smiled, bowing her head, then looking back up at him with her striking, violet eyes. A moment passed.

"Okay, I think we should…"

Before he could say exactly what he thought they should, Wiktoria reappeared, flushed and breathing heavily.

"Wiktoria?"

She didn't reply straight away, but instead grabbed her pack and started rummaging through it. Then she pulled out her breathing apparatus and looked up at them. "You need to see this."

Aecola and Lukasz looked at each other with alarm and promptly followed Wiktoria, grabbing their own breathing gear as they did so.

"What the hell?"

Lukasz pulled his breathing gear clumsily over his head, struggling for a minute to line up the tubing with his airways and blocking his own vision.

Aecola, still holding hers, didn't put it on, but took a tentative step forward to stand next to where Xin was watching a small deer in a clearing.

The deer stood, swaying slightly, every now and then taking half a step in a random direction, before stopping again. It didn't seem to be aware of the four humans watching it. A couple of these uncertain steps brought it around so that it was facing them.

Lukasz swore.

The creature's head was facing in their direction, but it was clear that it couldn't see them or, for that matter, anything else. Its eyes were completely misted over, just cloudy white orbs, around which was a crusted rim of some kind of discharge. The same discharge was accumulating around its mouth. It stood, swaying, for a moment, then lurched a step towards them.

All four of them instinctively stepped back.

"Is that...?"

Aecola, her face blanching, nodded. "Look at its coat," she pointed. When they peered at it, they could make out that the coat was discoloured in places, patches of greenish matter crusted on to the fur.

"It's infected," said Wiktoria.

"It is," Aecola confirmed.

Lukasz's voice, distorted through his breathing apparatus, asked, "Shouldn't you get your masks on?"

Wiktoria reached for hers, but Aecola put a hand on her arm. "It's okay. The poor thing's obviously ingested some of the spores. It's parasitic, keeping the deer alive long enough to wander off a certain distance before it dies. Then the fungus will grow in the body before it's ready to spore again. At this point it's horrible, but not an immediate threat. As long as you don't go over and try to pet it," she added.

"Fat chance," muttered Lukasz, shuddering.

"How far can it have wandered though, since ingesting the spores?" said Wiktoria.

Aecola glanced around the clearing but couldn't see any obvious sign of the fungus. She shook her head. "I don't know, but there's no sign of anything here. It's still the fruiting part of the fungus we need to look out for." She drew her bolt-pistol and, shaking only slightly, paused for a moment, staring at the defenceless creature that still seemed to be oblivious to their presence. Then she fired once, killing it.

"We need to burn the body."

Nobody slept much that night. After they burnt the carcass, they carried out a sweep of the immediate vicinity, carefully examining the trees and bushes for any sign of the fungus. After an hour or so, they reluctantly agreed that they were probably okay. Aecola would have carried on hiking through the night, that much was clear, but Lukasz put his foot down. "We've still three days to go, that's if we keep up our current pace. We start trying to push ourselves, we're going to stumble. Plus, I don't want to be pushing through undergrowth in the dark, not knowing what I'm brushing up against."

That argument, more than the pace, convinced Aecola. They set up their usual watch, but nobody got through an entire shift without someone else waking up, chatting for a while in low tones before trying to get back to sleep.

In the morning, Lukasz was more insistent than usual about breakfast. Knowing that none of them had slept well, he wanted them to be at least well-fed before the day's march.

They set off in grim spirits, Aecola leading. There was little chatter. By mid-morning, they became aware of an eerie stillness settling over the forest. When they stopped for lunch, Lukasz took Aecola to one side. "Are you sure we're heading in the right direction? It feels like we're heading into... something."

She pulled up the map on her datapad and accessed the internal compass. "There's nothing to suggest we're not. We've been right so far, and we've not deviated."

Lukasz looked around at the forest, concern showing on his face. There was precious little noise, no birdsong now. They hadn't seen any critters all morning. It even seemed to have gotten darker.

"Could it have spread farther than expected?"

"That was always a possibility. Depending on wind patterns, local ecology, atmosphere... it's going to react differently to every environment it lands on and the data we have on it is limited. Scientists have seen far more of the aftermath of infection than the process in action. We can't even guess at the mechanism by which it spreads from planet to planet." Aecola gave him a look that made it clear she wasn't happy about how little she knew. "I'm only a second-year ecology student, I've got no answers for you, Lukasz."

"No, I know. It's just so damned eerie. The sooner we get to Gran Palomos the better. Is it me, or is it getting darker?"

Aecola looked up. "I would expect the canopy to be getting slightly thicker, to be honest. We're descending, slightly, and there are going to be changes in the flora between our camp and Gran Palomos. If anything, that's a sign we're on the right track."

"Well, that's something."

Aecola nodded, half-heartedly.

After a hasty lunch of dried snack bars, the party pulled on their packs and started off again. An hour or so into the hike, Aecola halted them.

"Problem?"

"No, I was just thinking..." She was resting a palm on the trunk of a tree and looking up at it, thoughtfully. "I've been looking for a good, climbable tree. Thought I could take a shimmy up to the canopy, see if I can confirm our bearings. We might be able to see signs of Gran Palomos."

"Climb that?" Lukasz was incredulous.

She winked at him. "You forget, I've been out here climbing trees for months, Lukasz. All I needed was one with the right branch distribution."

He shrugged. "Fair enough then, let's take a break and let the jungle queen do her stuff."

They slipped out of their packs and Wiktoria took the opportunity to start brewing up some tea while Aecola took some kit out of her pack and attached it to her boots. "For extra grip." She put on her gloves as well, which were also specialised for climbing. Then, with a hand from Lukasz and Xin, she boosted herself up to the lowest branch and began her climb.

Lukasz and the others watched her for a bit then, as she got higher and Wiktoria's brew came to the boil, they let her get on with it and took their tea.

About twenty minutes later, they heard Aecola coming back down again. They watched her descend the final stretch, helping her down from the lowest branch back to the floor. She took a moment to catch her breath as they glanced uneasily between themselves. She did not look encouraged.

"Did you see it?"

"I didn't get up high enough."

"Branches not strong enough towards the top?"

Aecola shook her head. "Mycelium." She looked around at their anxious faces. "It's spreading along the canopy. I was right about the floral changes, but the darkness is being exacerbated by a network of mycelium. We're not seeing it down here, but we're in the infected zone. It's spreading up there."

"Shit." Lukasz rubbed his jaw. "How much danger are we in?"

Aecola shook her head. "It's not good. It's starting to develop fruiting bodies. Which, sooner or later, means spores."

"Shit," repeated Lukasz.

Aecola started pulling the spiked attachments from her boots. "We should move."

X

Any sense of caution began to be overtaken by anxiety. Aecola was pushing hard now, and Lukasz was less inclined to try and rein her in. The thought of lethal spores showering down at any moment was a horrifying one and the group buckled down and powered on through their tiredness. Eventually, though, they had to stop and once again it was Lukasz who called it. This time, Aecola really did look like she was going to argue, but her own weariness made her acknowledge that, as much as she hated it, she needed rest as much as any of them.

Again, they performed a careful sweep of the immediate area and this time Aecola also shimmied a short way up a few of the neighbouring trees. At one point, the others heard her curse and ran to the base of the tree she was currently climbing, but when she descended, she shook her head. "Nothing, I didn't see anything. Just caught my arm on a branch. Teach me to climb in the dark."

Wiktoria examined where she'd caught it. The skin was broken but it wasn't much more than a graze. She cleaned it and dressed it while Xin put a meal together.

The four of them sat round the all-purpose camp burner, enjoying the heat it gave off as it cooked their pre-packed meal pockets, and the friendly orange glow.

"So, the day after tomorrow?"

"Should be," said Aecola.

"Can't come too soon," said Wiktoria, quietly.

Xin flashed their fingers in agreement.

"With any luck, we should start coming out of the infected area tomorrow. We must be getting far enough away from the original site now," said Aecola, her voice full of artificial conviction, as if trying to convince herself as much as them.

"It's scary," said Lukasz, "but let's face it, all we've encountered is one infected deer and some early-stage fungal growth, right?" He looked to Aecola for confirmation. She nodded, tentatively, and he continued. "Realistically, we're still not in much danger. It's just a question of covering this last stretch, then we're done. We've seen no sign of the soldiers who're after us. We're doing okay."

"So far," said Wiktoria.

"Yeah, okay, so far," conceded Lukasz.

They turned in.

Xin was on watch when it happened. They shook Lukasz awake, then Wiktoria and Aecola. "People," they whispered, pointing in the direction from which they'd come.

The four moved instinctively. Pulling together their gear and returning it to their packs as quietly as they could, within moments they were ready to move out. Lukasz gave his instructions quickly and clearly, his voice low but deliberately over-annunciating to ensure he was understood. Xin and Aecola drew their bolt-pistols and then the four split up, Lukasz and Aecola creeping in one direction, Xin and Wiktoria in the other.

Rather than heading off in the direction of Gran Palomos, the two groups spread out to either side of the route they'd been hiking and backtracked slightly. If the soldiers had followed them this far, then they knew exactly where we're headed, Lukasz had reasoned. The safest option was to lay low and make room for them, hoping the soldiers would just press on and overtake them. The fact that they'd caught them meant, logically, they were moving faster. Let them overtake and hopefully that would be the last they saw of them.

What he didn't say, but was very conscious of himself, was that by doing that, it meant the soldiers were likely to be waiting for them when they got to town. That was, however, a problem for another day and he was starting to have a few ideas about that, too. In the meantime, the plan was to let them go on their way and have nothing to do with them.

They knew it was a small squad, so there was a limit to how spread out they could be. Creeping through the forest as quietly as they could, Lukasz and Aecola could hear the approaching people now. They weren't being as quiet as presumably they could be, which puzzled Lukasz. He guessed that the soldiers, used to night hiking and probably equipped with night-vision equipment, were taking their rest at some point during the day and were going all out at night, counting on coming upon the four of them while they were camped and letting surprise give them the advantage. *Luckily, we're more worried about you than you expected*, thought Lukasz.

Aecola tapped him lightly on the arm and, when he turned, pointed upwards. They were at the foot of a tree, one with low branches. Lukasz nodded, slinging the plasma rifle over his back and letting Aecola, as the better climber, give him a boost to one of the branches within reach. She pulled herself up behind him and the two of them, making as little noise as they could, ascended the tree until they were about twenty feet up. There, Lukasz settled himself with his back to the trunk, wedging himself in until he felt secure. He tried not to think about Aecola's body pressed against him on the branch and pulled his rifle around to watch the forest floor.

Xin and Wiktoria, meanwhile, had found a thick covering of bramble. Pausing for a moment to listen out for the soldiers, they judged themselves to have enough time and manoeuvred themselves into and under the bramble. They had light but durable jackets they'd brought from the ship, which proved to be resilient to the bramble's thorns. They could feel the plant scratching at them, but only through the material, which didn't give.

They waited, Xin with their bolt-pistol out and ready, Wiktoria with her staff beside her. For a minute or two, all they could hear was each other breathing. Then, Xin's fingers tapped out a quick rhythm. *Footsteps.*

The soldier was moving quietly, if not stealthily. Now that their eyes had become accustomed to the darkness, there was enough moonlight filtering through the canopy to allow them to see a short distance and so they were able to make him out as he approached.

He was wearing goggles, presumably for night vision, and carrying a pulse rifle. He wasn't in uniform, just anonymous camouflage gear, which settled the matter of whether he was one of the squad pursuing them. He was walking, rather than creeping, and at a decent pace. Xin's fingers moved again. *Must be hoping to catch us asleep.* Wiktoria nodded.

There was a tense moment when the soldier stopped, not more than five feet from where they were hidden. Wiktoria held her breath, but then slowly let it out again as the soldier slung his rifle over his shoulder, unfastened his trousers and started to urinate against a tree. He was finishing up when he put a hand to his ear.

"No," he said quietly. "Nothing. Stopped for a piss."

So, the soldiers were split up but in radio contact. Presumably not so far apart but allowing them to cover a wider track. Xin tapped her again. *Lukasz right. Know where we're going. Assumed straight line.*

Lukasz was right. And now, if he'd made the right call, the soldiers would sweep through and ahead of them. Wiktoria longed to creep out and take this one by surprise, push the odds further in their favour, but as Lukasz had pointed out, if they did that, they'd be giving up their location and the remainder would close in on them in no time. Better to let them pass and hope that was the last they saw of them. These were trained soldiers and, with the best will in the world, the four of them would be hopelessly outclassed if it came to any kind of combat situation.

The soldier refastened his trousers and, wiping his hands on his thighs, carried on and past them.

They spent the rest of the night in their hiding place, alternating watches. When the sun came up, they emerged from under the bramble. It was four hours or so since the soldier had passed by and there had been no sign of them since. They made their way back to their original camp, where Lukasz and Aecola were waiting for them.

"All clear?"

"Yeah, no problems," replied Lukasz. "Had a bit of a scare when one passing near us thought his mate had seen something. Think they had some way of tracking each other and one of them had stopped, but it turned out he was just taking a leak."

"That was our guy," said Wiktoria and she recounted how they feared they had been spotted until the soldier had relieved himself.

"They seemed in a hurry," said Aecola.

"They know they have time to make up and no idea where we are. I guess they have to account for the fact that we could still be headed somewhere other than Gran Palomos, so need to get there and see what's what before thinking about alternatives. It's a huge forest; they must be flailing desperately."

"I'm surprised they're not better trackers. We're doing our best, but I find it hard to believe we're covering our tracks that well."

"It's a question of time. They might have tracked us so far but needed to catch up. Once they knew where we were going, they would assume we'd be taking the most direct route and switched to hiking at night in the hopes of catching us unawares."

"Yeah," said Wiktoria, "guess you were right about that."

"So now they're ahead of us and if they're resting during the day, how do we make sure we don't trip over them?" asked Aecola.

"They're making better time than we are. We'll go carefully, but they've just had four hours hiking, so we're not going to reach where they are now for at least four hours, probably more. It depends when they've fixed their rest cycles, of course but with any luck, by then they'll be even further ahead of us. We won't catch them now."

"I'm hearing a lot about luck and assumptions," remarked Aecola, nervously.

Lukasz flashed her what he hoped was a winning smile.

"It's our best asset."

XI

Petru called a halt and the squad converged on where he had stopped. It was a couple of hours after dawn, and they'd been marching all night.

"Any sign?" he asked. It was a pointless question; they were all in radio contact. He'd have known already if any of them had seen anything, but he was very discomforted. The tracking had been a slow business, so when their maps had suggested Gran Palomos as the only place the targets could conceivably be heading, he'd decided to speed up and hope his hunch paid off. After all, it's not like the four of them could sweep the whole forest and, if the targets had any sense, they'd have worked in a few false trails, and they didn't have the time to lose following even one.

His men shook their heads. They looked exhausted; he'd been pushing them hard. Tyger was rubbing at his throat, still bruised from where one of the activists had struck him at the ambush. At least the cut on his head was healing up. Jekk and Goff were in better shape, although all four men were inwardly seething. Not only had this bitch escaped them a second time, but now she'd hooked up with another group of activists. On top of that, Zane was dead, shot in the back by one of these bastards. Goff was seasoned enough to know that missions like this could go south but Petru was aware that the other two, especially Jekk, were starting to show signs of blaming him for the failure. Trouble was brewing. They needed a win, and quickly.

"Okay, we'll take a couple of hours here before we press on. Goff, you're on first watch."

Goff nodded while the other three men dropped their packs and lay down. He waited until the three were asleep, which didn't take long, before securing himself a position nearby to keep watch from.

There was a noise, out in the forest ahead of them. Goff didn't move, but his senses sprung to attention, ears straining. Something was moving through the undergrowth. Not fast, and not quietly. And it was coming toward them.

He frowned. It was making a lot of noise for an animal, but it was unlikely to be a person, surely. The kids they were following shouldn't be coming in this direction and there was no reason for anyone else to be out here. Unless they'd got separated. One of them got injured, maybe? Or lost? And was now heading in the wrong direction, right into their arms.

Licking his lips, Goff raised his rifle and centred it on the part of the forest the sound was coming from. Then he tapped his earpiece. "Sir, incoming."

The three sleeping men stirred and looked around for Goff. Petru saw him first. Goff held up a finger, gestured to where the sound was coming from, then held his finger to his lips.

The three men reached quietly for their weapons and spread out, crouching down for cover. They could all hear the approaching sound now. Petru tapped his earpiece and whispered, "Alive, men, if at all possible."

A figure lurched into view. It was a man, so not the girl, but possibly one of her group. He certainly looked familiar, although none of them had got a good look at the others that Aecola was now travelling with. The man was stumbling, haphazardly, seemingly paying little attention to where he was going. Before he reached them, he paused, swaying as he stood, his head looking one way, then another.

"He looks drunk," whispered Tyger.

Petru frowned. Drunk or not, his men should know better than to give themselves away with idle chatter. He was painfully aware that their failure to apprehend the girl was starting to impact not only morale, but also discipline.

The man did look drunk though. He was swaying as if he could collapse at any moment and there was something decidedly odd about the way his head was moving around, as if he was looking but not seeing anything.

Petru's heart chilled. He suddenly got an inkling of why the man looked so familiar. Bringing his rifle up to his shoulder, he looked at the man through the scope.

He was right, the man couldn't see anything. His eyes were misted over, cloudy. He wasn't turning his head to look. Maybe to hear, but not to look. What sent ice through Petru's veins was the man's wound that he could now see. A headwound, the flesh burnt and cauterized, as if he'd been shot from close range by a bolt-pistol. That was impossible, though. With a wound like that the man would be dead.

He'd certainly been dead, the last time Petru had seen him.

Yoak still stood where he'd stopped, swaying and turning his head. His eyes and mouth were both leaking discharge, crusting up at the corners. His skin was yellowing, with greenish tinges here and there. The green patches looked crusty, scabrous.

Jekk swore, taking a hand off his rifle as he rubbed at his eyes and tried to make sense of what he was seeing.

"Is that…" Goff started to say.

Petru stood and, holding his rifle ready, took a few steps towards the swaying scientist, swallowing down his own disquiet. Behind him, he heard his men get to their feet. Ahead of him, Yoak stopped moving his head and instead turned to face Petru, his unseeing eyes seeming to peer somewhere over the soldier's left shoulder.

"Stay back, men," ordered Petru, needlessly. None of the soldiers had the slightest desire to get any closer. "Yoak?"

The scientist, swaying slightly, moved his head a fraction, as if trying to pinpoint the noise.

"Yoak, is that you?"

The man's mouth opened, but nothing came out. The dry, cracked skin at the corners of his mouth gave and blood started to trickle down his jaw. He lurched forward a couple of paces before stopping again.

"Yoak, can you hear me?"

The mouth opened again and Petru could just hear a deathly hiss, barely perceptible. The thing that had been Yoak took another couple of steps, this time prompting Petru to retreat the same distance.

"Yoak, don't move. You've got some kind of infection. You need to keep back."

Yoak hissed again, then reached forward with both arms and lifted a foot, only to be blown back by a pulse rifle blast to his chest. The body flew back and crumpled on the floor.

Petru spun around to see which of his men had fired.

"S-sorry, Captain," stammered Tyger. He was sweating and his skin was deathly pale. "I panicked..." All three of his men looked sick and right at that moment Petru realised Tyger might have just saved his life. He nodded, slowly, and turned back to where Yoak's body was lying on the ground, twitching, its hands still reaching for something it couldn't see.

"What the hell happened to him?" asked Jekk.

Petru shook his head. "I don't want to know."

But he had an idea.

Wiktoria nudged Lukasz, gesturing ahead to where Aecola was leading the hike. "She's doing it again."

That was the fourth or fifth time Wiktoria had seen Aecola scratch at her arm where she'd caught it climbing the night before.

"So, tell her to stop," said Lukasz, irritably. He was starting to get jumpy, thinking of nothing so much as how soon they could get out of this damned forest.

"I did, but she just looked at me like I was fussing."

"Aren't you?"

"Lukasz, an infection out here wouldn't be good at the best of times. If she opens it up while this fungus is about, I hate to think what she might expose herself to."

"Okay, so take a look at it when we stop, put a fresh dressing on it."

Wiktoria bit back a response of frustration. Aecola would listen to Lukasz more than she would anyone else, that much was obvious. Wiktoria had seen the way the girl looked up to the pilot. Wiktoria could really do with him taking that on board right now.

They hiked on.

Ahead of them, Petru called his men to a halt again, ignoring their grumbles as they converged on him. He instead pointed at something on a tree limb, something white and wispy, almost like a cobweb.

"Anyone seen anything like that?"

The men shrugged. "I don't know, Captain, maybe."

They were even more sullen now, the confrontation with Yoak having stirred them all up and, what's worse, Petru couldn't even blame them. He wanted nothing more himself than to get out of this bloody forest and off this wretched planet, even if it meant reporting a mission failure. He'd seen plenty of active duty before, fighting insurrectionists on Ehoatror, putting down an uprising on Friginata, but nothing as unnerving as this. Men, he could kill. This was something else entirely.

"There's more over here, sir."

Goff was pointing at another tree.

Petru swore. He pulled a small pouch from his pack and handed each of his men a small, black device that looked like a diver's mouthpiece.

Jekk protested. "Is that really necessary, Captain? Those things make me gag. Who's going to be using gas out here?"

"It's for the fungus," snapped Petru. "Unless you want to end up like Yoak, use it. That's an order."

Tyger and Goff both took one. Jekk stared down at the one Petru held out to him for a moment, before grudgingly reaching out and taking it. He swallowed a couple of times, looking down at the contraption in his hand, then quickly rammed it into his mouth. He screwed his eyes up as he worked it into place, then gave Petru a pointed look.

Petru returned his look with a curt nod, then put his own breathing device in.

It was just after midday when Wiktoria held up a hand. "Aecola, wait."

She stopped, turning back to the others. "What is…"

Wiktoria held a finger to her lips. "Listen."

The four of them waited a moment, Aecola unconsciously scratching at her arm.

"Off to the left somewhere, an animal in distress?"

Something was thrashing about in the undergrowth. Every now and then it would stop, as if it had worn itself out, and then it would start up again.

"We're in a hurry," said Lukasz, taking a step forward but Aecola stopped him.

"Good catch, Wiktoria. With everything going on, we ought to check it out. It may be important."

Lukasz sighed. "I thought you were in more of a hurry than the rest of us."

"I am," said Aecola firmly, "so let's get on with it."

She headed off towards the sound.

It didn't take long to find the source of the noise. In a nearby clearing they came across a man lying on his back. He was thrashing about as if trying to right himself but didn't seem to have the required control over his own limbs.

Wiktoria went to take a step closer, but Aecola grabbed her arm firmly. "Don't go near him."

"He needs help."

"I think he's beyond help," said Lukasz.

Wiktoria looked at the man on the floor. "Oh no..."

Sure enough, the man was exhibiting a lot of the same symptoms as the deer they'd found the day before yesterday, the misted-over eyes, the discolouration on his skin. On top of which he also had one pulse burn in his chest and what looked like another in his head.

"How is he alive?" asked Lukasz

Xin whispered, "I'm not sure he is."

Lukasz shuddered.

"Xin's right," said Aecola. "We know of other species of fungus with parasitic capabilities, the ability for the fungus to invade the brain stem and actually control physical movement."

"To the point of animating the dead?" asked Lukasz, his voice full of dread.

"Well, not anything I've come across, but this is... this is all beyond me. There's no saying what it's capable of."

Aecola pulled the breathing apparatus from her pack, prompting the others to do the same, and put it on. "I think we should keep this on until we're well clear of the infected zone now."

"And what about your arm?" said Wiktoria.

"My arm?"

Wiktoria pointed at the dressing. "You've been scratching that all day."

"Okay, okay. Let's burn this and when we get away, I'll let you look at it."

There was no mistaking it now. The further Petru and his men walked, the more obvious the signs of infection. As well as the mycelium working its way down the tree trunks, there were now sporocarps forming, bright yellow blobs about six inches across. Out of necessity, the soldiers' speed was now reduced as they tried to avoid coming into contact with the increased amount of fungal life on the plants around them.

"This is so messed up," complained Jekk, his voice on the verge of cracking, as he used the butt of his rifle to hold a branch back out of his way.

"Focus, Jekk," came Petru's voice in his earpiece. "Getting to Gran Palomos is now not only our best shot at catching the fugitive, but also of getting out of this shit, so let's just get on and get out, yeah?"

"Yes Captain," muttered the soldier, his shaved scalp glistening with sweat, a result of the constant tension they were now under.

It was not only deathly quiet in the forest now, but it was also palpably gloomier. Shards of light burst through the canopy, proving it was still daylight up there, but the gaps between the foliage were now more widely dispersed and the cover was thicker. More than that, the light had a strange, sickly hue, deathlike. It didn't take much imagination to work out what was up there keeping the light out.

They pressed on, until Petru called for another break.

"We'll take four hours here. That should take us to nightfall, then we can press on. They can't be that far ahead of us now."

"Four hours? Just sitting in this nightmare?"

Petru took a step towards Jekk, physically emphasising the chain of command. "We rest properly, we move quicker. We just carry on indefinitely, we make mistakes, then one of us winds up dead."

Jekk just stared back, sullenly.

Still eyeballing Jekk, Petru told Tyger to take the first watch. Tyger didn't protest.

The wound was small, barely more than a scratch, but there was no overlooking the greenish tinge to the skin around the opening.

"This doesn't look good, Aec."

"Then we need to press on. The sooner we get to Gran Palomos, the sooner I can get this flushed." Something in her voice sounded off, more than just the distortion from the breathing apparatus that was affecting them all.

Wiktoria looked up at Lukasz, who shrugged. "She's right, we can't do anything about it out here. Getting out of the forest and back to civilisation solves all our problems. Staying here does nothing."

Wiktoria pulled a fresh dressing from her kit along with some medi-wipes. She cleaned the wound as best she could, then redressed it.

"Try to avoid scratching it, Aecola."

The student nodded vaguely, then stood up. Xin helped her shoulder her pack as the group started off.

Jekk shook Petru awake. "It's time, sir."

Petru ran a hand over his face then checked his watch. "Hold it," he said quietly, seeing Jekk go to wake the others. He adjusted the mouthpiece that had slipped as he slept, pushing into his cheek.

"Sir?" The soldier's face was pale, tired looking. There was little trace of the angry resentment he'd exhibited earlier.

"Jekk, I understand why you're frustrated. I know this mission has proved problematic, and a lot more dangerous than we were led to believe, but our best shot at getting this done and ourselves out of here is to work together. I could shout and pull rank, and I will if I must, but it'll be a lot more effective if we just come together as a squad."

Jekk paused, seemingly considering the captain's words. Then he rubbed a hand over his scalp and nodded. "Okay, sir. Point taken."

"Good man. Get the others up."

The two parties hiked on, the one in front chasing the one behind. The forest was eerily silent and gloomy now, the eight hikers marching quietly, each lost in their own thoughts. The soldiers, with their pulse rifles at the ready and their state-of-the-art breathing apparatus, all now wishing they hadn't been assigned this mission. Aecola was dreading running into the soldiers before they reached Gran Palomos. Under their breathing masks, the crew of the *Tethree* were all wondering how quickly they'd be off this planet and back in space. Wiktoria kept an anxious eye on Aecola, but the student seemed to be taking the instruction not to scratch her wound seriously.

As it approached nightfall, Lukasz called their group to a halt.

"Okay, so we've not run into them all day. If they carry on hiking by night then this is where they should disappear out of our reckoning altogether, at least until we reach Gran Palomos."

"And what happens then?" asked Wiktoria.

"I've been thinking about that. Once the data's uploaded then they've no cause to pursue you, right?" Lukasz turned to Aecola.

She didn't seem to register that he was speaking to her.

"Right, Aecola?"

She looked at him blankly, then shook her head, as if to clear away the cobwebs.

"I guess not," she said, finally.

"And if they haven't seen us, not properly anyway, then the three of us can circle the town, come in from the far side and they won't even be looking for us. We walk in, find somewhere to upload the data, their mission's over. We can then come and get you, get your wound looked at and it's all done."

"You make it sound straightforward," said Aecola.

"Yeah, well, I'm not offering any guarantees, but I don't see any glaring holes."

"We're resting here then?"

Lukasz looked around. "Seems as good a place as any. You want to check it out?"

They split up again, Wiktoria and Xin sweeping the immediate area for signs of the soldiers, while Aecola and Lukasz set about climbing a couple of the trees to see how the mycelium situation was looking.

When they reconvened, the news was better than they'd hoped. There was no sign of anyone in the nearby vicinity. What's more, they'd found what looked like signs the soldiers had already passed by this way. As for the mycelium, it was noticeably more thinly spread in this part of the forest. Lukasz hadn't even needed Aecola to tell him that.

"So, we're coming out of the infected zone?" asked Wiktoria.

"We must be." With relief, Aecola pulled off her breathing kit, running a hand through her knotted, unkempt hair. "We're only a day's hike or so away from Gran Palomos now, it's already spread farther than I thought possible. If we're not coming out of the zone now, we're never getting the town evacuated in time."

"How could it have got so far?" The others followed her lead in removing their breathing masks.

"You saw the deer, and that poor man. It only needed a convenient carrier, and it could conceivably have jumped the expected dispersal pattern by miles."

"Let's hope it hasn't latched on to too many others," said Lukasz.

"I think we should be okay in that respect," replied Aecola thoughtfully. "Judging by the blast wounds, the man was probably already dead, or at least dying, a sitting duck for the fungus to take hold, and the same might be true of the deer. I can't help feeling if it was finding a lot of carriers, we would have seen more signs of it. More corpses, more infected animals. Maybe it needs an incapacitated host to access."

"I guess that makes sense. We've certainly not seen any other bodies or anything," agreed Wiktoria. "How's the arm?"

Aecola gave her a wan smile. "Itches like crazy, but I'm trying to resist."

"Good job. You want me to redress it?"

"Maybe not now, I just want to get some sleep and I think disturbing it will just set it off. You can change it in the morning before we start."

Xin's fingers danced.

"Yep, tomorrow, probably by mid-afternoon," replied Lukasz.

Even Xin looked relieved by that forecast.

"Lukasz, Lukasz…"

Lukasz groaned. Another day, another panicked awakening.

"What is it?"

"Aecola, she's gone."

He sat up in a flash, staring at Wiktoria. "What do you mean, gone?"

"She was on watch. I woke up, realised it was after the time she should have got me to relieve her and when I looked for her, she was… gone."

XII

Aecola had been feeling peculiar all day. Slightly... disconnected. She still worried about the soldiers, and the fungus, but somehow it all seemed remote, intangible. Not quite of the moment. As if the events she was experiencing were in fact just memories of things that had already happened.

When she had climbed the tree at the spot they had chosen to camp down in, she had indeed found the mycelium to be more thinly spread around the treetops and, for that matter, higher up. When she found it, however, it hadn't made her shudder the way it had before. She'd had to stop herself reaching out and touching it, the thin white strands looked so... harmless. Pretty, even. Indeed, she had half reached out and it was only the sight of the dressing on her infected wound that had brought her to her senses. Shaking her head to clear her mind, she had shimmied back down the tree and reported what she'd seen, leaving out the part about how she had reacted to it.

The others seemed relieved, but she could only wonder at the fact that she didn't share that relief. Not that she didn't think they were getting out of the infected zone, nor was she lying when she made the observation about the lack of active carriers they'd encountered and what that implied. It was just that it all seemed... less important to her than it did to them.

She was tired, that must be it. She'd kept up a strong pace for days and now that they were reaching Gran Palomos, her body was probably reaching the end of the reserves it had been parcelling out for her. She was the first one asleep and Xin had, at first, struggled to wake her for her watch. There was still heat coming from the pot, so she made herself a cup of coffee as she watched Xin pull their blanket up over themselves.

Aecola...

She looked around but the others were sound asleep. Wind in the trees? It had sounded like her name, but she knew she was jittery. She put it out of her mind.

She stood up and quietly paced a circuit of the camp, sipping at her coffee and trying to prod her mind into full wakefulness, rolling her neck to work out a crick she'd got from sleeping on the ground. She was conscious of her arm starting to itch again but pushed the thought out of her head.

Aecola...

Again, she ignored the sound that she continued to tell herself was only in her head. She looked over at where the three figures were laying around the mobile heat source, her gaze lingering a moment longer on Lukasz. She was glad she wasn't alone in the forest, which she could quite easily have been at this point. They seemed like good people, and it had made this journey a lot less daunting. Lukasz, especially, seemed kind. Xin was a little unnerving, but even they seemed friendly in their own way. She felt as if she could trust them.

Can you...?

This time, she spun around. Not just her name, but a direct response to her thoughts. She whispered, tentatively, "Who's there?"

There was no reply.

Somewhere off in the forest, Aecola realised she could now see a faint, greenish glow. She frowned. Was that the direction from which the voice was coming? What was it? It wasn't fire and it didn't look manmade. She took a few steps towards the light, then paused, waiting to hear if the voice came back.

Nothing.

She glanced back at the three forms on the forest floor. They seemed okay and it really was unlikely that the soldiers were going to come back on themselves now, so it wouldn't hurt just to go and investigate the light, would it? There was no need to wake anybody, she'd only be gone a few minutes.

The light got brighter remarkably quickly; it did suggest it was very close. Aecola put a hand to her head, squinting. It wasn't that the light was so bright, but it was... intense? Her head was starting to spin a little. Maybe she should go back and wake Lukasz.

She didn't, though, stepping forward and into a small clearing. The light was definitely emanating from here, although there was no obvious source. It was more that this clearing was just... lighter? It made no sense. Aecola shook her head, now fuzzy from the intense light of the clearing. Without even realising she was doing it, she put a hand to her arm, scratching lightly at her injury.

A small deer wandered out into the clearing from the trees and looked up at her.

Aecola...

Aecola started, almost tripping over as she took a step back.

It was the same deer from a few days ago, the infected one, she was sure of it. The same dead eyes, the same crusted discharge and matted fur. But they had burned that one, hadn't they? This must be a different deer.

Aecola...

"What do you want?" she whispered. Was it the deer talking? Its mouth didn't appear to move but the way it looked up at her suggested intent... She shook her head, this was absurd. She should go back to the camp and wake Wiktoria, get her wound checked out. She didn't move.

We want your help...

"I don't understand. Help with what? Who are you?"

Aecola...

"I don't understand!" she repeated.

Aecola, we need you...

Aecola turned a full circle, staring up at the trees. The voice seemed to come from all around her. It grew somehow warm, protective. She was still confused, but she wasn't fearful. The voice somehow reminded her of her mother.

The trees leant in, their branches shaking and reaching for her, but not to harm her. No, they were beckoning her, calling her to their embrace.

Aecola, we are the forest...

The forest, yes! The forest that she had been protecting, that she had bonded with and fought for and wanted to save. It knew her! It recognised her! It knew what she was there to do!

Aecola, you must come...

Aecola, beaming from ear to ear, looked down and saw that her clothes had changed. She was in a green cotton dress, floaty and light. She spun in it, delighting at the way that it flew up and out. It was beautiful.

Aecola, you must come...

Still spinning, she jolted to a stop as she realised that behind her, a small group of figures were approaching her, slowly. They were faceless, dressed all in green and hooded.

"Are you the forest?"

Go with them, Aecola, they will guide you...

Aecola followed the figures through the trees. They didn't speak and she didn't try to talk to them. The forest had told her to go with them, so go with them she must. Whether they chose to speak to her or not was their choice, she knew. She only needed to do as she was told.

She held out her hands as she walked, brushing her fingers against the trunks of the trees they passed, feeling their leaves dance on her hands. The sun was coming up now and for what seemed like the first time in days, sunlight, true golden sunlight, was breaking through the canopy, illuminating here and there patches of the forest floor. As she walked through one beam of light, she pirouetted, loving the feel of the warmth on her skin.

One of the figures she followed, seemingly sensing that she had stopped, turned around and reached out for her. Where before there had been no face beneath the hood of its green robe, there was now a mouth. Just a mouth; and it opened, hissing a wordless, sibilant sound.

Follow it, Aecola...

The figure turned away and carried on walking through the forest. Aecola followed.

She could hear birds now, chittering in the trees. The forest was alive and responding to her as she was led through it by her silent guides. Every now and then, one of them would disappear, their form dissipating into smoke, but always a new one would appear, or rather, she would become aware of it, in a way that suggested it had always been there, she just hadn't seen it before.

Once, she tried to reach out and touch the cloak of the nearest figure. It eluded her, ducking away from her hand, and leering back at her with the same, wordless hiss. It didn't seem threatening but there was a warning in the way it hissed, its eyeless face conveying, in a way Aecola could not describe, the suggestion that all would be well if she just continued to follow. But her actions, so far as they pertained to the creatures, should only consist of following meekly, lest their wrath be awakened. She sensed a raw power in the creatures, a primeval, natural power that although harnessed for good, could strike out in temper and she withdrew her hand, holding it close to her chest.

The creature turned back and carried on its way.

They seemed to walk for hours, through forest that shone in the light of the Netaran sun. The trees seemed to step aside for their group, allowing great, wide shafts of sunlight to illuminate their path. Here and there were flowers; great patches of tiny blue flowers; small, concentrated groupings of pink blooms; single tall-stemmed yellow orchids. Aecola was delighted by their fragrance. She called out to her guides to stop so that she might smell them a while. One of the green figures turned and held a finger to where its mouth would be. Another beckoned her on.

And on. And on, they walked. Occasionally the trees would part so far as to open out into a meadow.

Go on, Aecola, dance...

She danced in the meadow, spinning and running her hands through the flowers, until two of the figures in green floated back to her and took hold of her in a grasp she couldn't feel, pulling her towards the trees at the far side of the meadow.

She let herself be pulled, her mouth open in wonder as a cloud of small, orange butterflies flew past.

"It's so beautiful..."

Hurry, Aecola, hurry. For this beauty would be ours...

By the trees, the figures in green slowly let themselves drop to the floor, their hoods covering their faceless heads as they bowed at the neck. Aecola knelt among them. They passed her food... such food! Small, delicate cakes, rich in flavour; the sweetest bread; fruit bursting with ripeness. Such food as she had never tasted on Netaris, or even Ekkaris, washed down with the sweetest wine.

After she had eaten, she laid back on the mossy floor and slept.

When she awoke, Aecola was momentarily confused. "Where am I? Lukasz?"

There is no Lukasz...

She shook her head. The voice was right; now she thought on it, the name meant nothing to her. A memory of a dream, perhaps.

It was still light, but the sun was descending in the sky. Around her, the faceless figures in green stood in a circle, holding hands. Except she could see no hands, just the meeting of their robes at the end of their arms.

The forest had changed again, the trees looked foreboding, overwhelming. Something in the way their bark was patterned looked threatening, malicious even.

It turns on us, we must flee it, Aecola...

The figures in green started to float away from her.

Don't leave them, they are your Guardians...

She ran after them.

The forest had indeed changed. Where the trees had reached for her lovingly before, now they snatched at her, pulling at her dress. The birdsong had morphed into the barking calls of carrion birds, hungry for Aecola's flesh. The ground stabbed at her feet and the bushes tore at her arms. A branch lashed out at her face, tearing at her cheek.

Ahead of her, the figures smoked out of existence and popped up again with ever increasing frequency. Sometimes, they would float apart, almost out of sight, and she would cry out for them, begging them to wait. They seemed to pay her no mind, yet she never lost sight of them. They would regroup as quickly as they had split apart, like a murmuration of birds.

The scent of flowers had evaporated, leaving just the smell of rotting vegetation and the occasional tang of dead flesh.

Aecola tripped, falling flat on the forest floor where she lay, winded, watching as the bugs and burrowing things of the forest ran out to see what had shaken their homes. She squealed, pushing herself up and frantically brushing at her arms. A worm, thick and pink, unwrapped itself from around her finger and dropped to the ground.

A green figure appeared at her shoulder and, once more in that way that she could not feel, took hold of her and propelled her forward, gliding beside her as she ran, holding her up.

Now it rained, a thick and heavy rain that soaked through her green dress and made it cling to her body. The green figures, her companions, almost disappeared amid the rainfall, their insubstantial forms seemingly melting away, leaving just the impression of their presence. Aecola called out to them, running faster until she had caught them.

They turned to face her, all of them now mouthed, and they hissed in unison.

Danger... Run with us... We must run...

She nodded, crying a little, feeling like a small child and wishing she was home on... she shook her head, home on... She couldn't recall the name. She tried to picture her mother and father but all she could see in her mind were two figures, faceless, dressed in green.

How long had she been running in the forest? Hours? Days? Her whole life?

Were these companions in green her parents? Her family?

Was she them?

Were they her?

The rain continued to fall.

Run, Aecola...

She ran.

Her guides led her straight and true, never deviating. At times, they seemed to run almost through trees, so straight now was their path that they allowed nothing to turn them from their course. She followed as best she could, sometimes stumbling, sometimes getting pulled back by the branches of mischievous trees, looking to catch her, to thwart her escape. But she managed to keep running, following the figures in green until, all at once, the trees gave way.

The green figures stood at the top of a long, gentle slope that led down to a road that, as she followed it with her eyes, led to a city! A wondrous city of towers and spires, all of glass. It glistened like a jewel, a beautiful, dreadful jewel.

All at once, Aecola longed to be back in the forest. Even the dark and malevolent forest seemed preferable to this alien and mysterious thing, this artificial dwelling place of man.

But you have a mission, Aecola...

"I can't," she whispered. "I can't."

You must spread my message, Aecola. They must all know me, through you...

She started to weep.

"Don't make me! I can't! Don't make me!"

One of the figures in green, towering over her, opened its dreadful mouth.

"You musssst..."

Aecola screamed.

XIII

Lukasz started as Wiktoria put her hand gently on his arm. "We'll find her," she said quietly. He nodded but didn't say anything in response, just took another sip of his coffee.

At first, when they had awoken to find Aecola gone, he hadn't known what to do. They had so little time to waste, yet they could hardly leave her behind, not with the infection working its way through her body.

A search of the immediate area had turned up nothing. She'd taken nothing with her except the clothes she stood up in. Her datapad, with its internal compass attuned to Netaris' magnetic field and, more critically, the recording of the release of the fungus, was still in her pack. It was like she had just vanished.

In the end, the only thing to do was to press on. To sit waiting for her wasn't an option. To split up and widen the search would be too time-consuming with just the three of them. They would have to press on to Gran Palomos, hoping that Aecola had also left in that direction and that they could catch her up. Failing that, they would have to find an uplink, get her recording to the university themselves and then report her missing and try and get the local authorities to search for her. Lukasz hadn't forgotten the need to get medical attention for Litton either and that, in the end, forced their hand.

A hard hike had finally brought them to the forest edge by nightfall and the lights of Gran Palomos could just be made out across the plain. Lukasz had hated being that close and not just finishing the trek but, without Aecola, they knew little of what might be on the plain in front of them. Reluctantly, they retreated a short way into the forest to make camp. Gran Palomos would have to wait until morning.

Xin looked up as Wiktoria walked back into the camp.

"He's fine, just finishing his coffee."

Xin nodded and continued to pack up their gear, now divided three ways instead of four. They double-checked Aecola's datapad and secured it inside their jacket. Sweeping up their hair into their hood, they tied their scarf over their mouth and then hoisted their pack up onto their back. Wiktoria did the same with hers and then grabbed Lukasz's. The pulse rifle they'd taken from the soldier they left behind. One less person needed one less weapon and, besides, bolt-pistols could be hidden inside a jacket but there was no hiding a high spec military-issue rifle. Now that they were heading into civilisation, they couldn't afford the attention that would bring.

The grassy plain made for easy hiking, as it turned out. The ground undulated somewhat but posed no serious problems. Were it not for their concern over Aecola, the walk would have been quite enjoyable. Certainly, being out in full sunshine, away from the forest, made for a pleasant change. Being further from the deadly fungus that, even now, was spreading through the forest behind them was even more of a relief.

A couple of hours into the hike, they came across a dusty track that seemed to be heading in the same direction as they were. Lukasz halted the march, pulling a water bottle from his pack and taking a long swig, before splashing some on his face and the back of his neck.

"What do you think?" he asked.

"We'll make quicker time if we follow it," replied Wiktoria. "On the other hand, we may increase our chances of running into the soldiers. Without Aecola, however, we don't even know that they have any idea who we are. And we'll look less suspicious taking the track than we would avoiding it."

Xin, with a flash of fingers, agreed.

"Yeah, that's what I thought. Come on, then."

As they walked on along the track, it soon joined with a larger road. Then they came across fences, and cattle within the fences. They stopped briefly to check the closest animals for any sign of infection, of which there was none.

It was an hour or so before midday when they heard an engine. They were still a good few hours from Gran Palomos, Lukasz estimated, although while the town had been a beacon at night from their vantage point on the forest's edge, crossing the plain by day meant they had no real sense of how far it was now, as it was totally out of sight.

The three resisted the urge to hide, relying again on being unknown to the soldiers pursuing Aecola. They walked on and then, a few minutes later, stepped onto the verge as the engine noise swelled behind them, announcing the arrival of a dilapidated old truck.

The truck pulled up beside them and a face appeared at the window and said something to them in a language none of them recognised. They stared back at him, blankly.

"Hello," said the old man at the wheel of the truck, when he realised that the three kids hadn't understood him.

"Hey," said Lukasz.

"You need lift?"

"Are you going to Gran Palomos?"

"Gran Palomos? No. My farm. It's not far from Gran Palomos. Save you time."

Lukasz looked at the other two. Xin shrugged. Wiktoria gave a cautious nod.

"Thank you."

The old man pointed at the rear of the truck and the three walked around to climb aboard. Lukasz, ahead of the other two, grabbed hold of the tailboard and heaved himself up, swinging a leg over. It was all he could do to keep moving and not freeze in terror at the sight of the four armed men already sat in the rear of the truck.

It had happened just as they were leaving the forest and heading down onto the plain. In their relief at having escaped the forest, the men had let their guard down somewhat and one misstep saw Tyger sprawling on the floor. The others laughed, until he tried to get up and fell right back down again, yelping at the pain shooting up his leg.

"I don't think it's broken," said Goff. "Likely just a sprain. It's going to be hell to walk on though."

Petru cursed. As if enough things hadn't gone wrong on this damned mission already. For a moment, he considered just leaving Tyger there but, after his speech to Jekk about pulling together, leaving him now would just about do it for his command.

"It's okay, Captain, I can walk on..." Tyger interrupted himself with another yelp of pain as he tried again to stand.

"Tyger, take it easy! Just hold on a minute."

Tyger lowered himself back down to the ground gingerly.

"Jekk, run back up to the treeline, find a decent branch that we can make a crutch out of. Goff, there should be a road down there off to the east. It takes us a little out of the way, but it ends up back on the route to Gran Palomos. I've no idea how busy it is. Might be nobody on it but see what it looks like and what our chances of getting picked up are."

"Sir." The two men left.

"I'm sorry, Captain," said Tyger.

"Not your fault, Tyger," said Petru, wearily. "It was just an accident."

Accident or another part of some sort of curse. Petru at this point was undecided.

Petru groaned when the old man pulled over again. It wasn't that getting a ride hadn't been a relief, but the old farmer seemed to be in no hurry to get anywhere. An indigenous native, they had been unable to communicate their urgency to him and so had waited as he had stopped in at two other farms on the way back to his own which, he had assured them, would put them in hobbling distance of Gran Palomos. By now, not even Petru was thinking about the girl. He'd more or less assumed that they were never catching her before she reached an uplink, and he was expecting to get the evac signal at any moment. The mission was a bust and, right now, all he wanted was a hot shower and a cold beer.

And not necessarily in that order.

"At least it's not a farm this time," said Goff, when he realised they had just pulled up at the side of the road. Voices, muffled by the canvas cover they were sat under, could be heard from the side.

"Old man stopped to talk to another of his friends no doubt," grumbled Jekk. "Can't we just kick him out and take his truck?" he suggested for the third time. Petru didn't bother replying.

Tyger, asleep with the aid of painkillers now that he didn't have to walk, snorted in his sleep and tried to roll over.

After a brief conversation between the old man and whoever he'd stopped for, a pair of hands grabbed hold of the tailboard and a foot appeared as a young man hauled himself into the back of the truck. He looked momentarily surprised to see them but didn't stop as he pulled himself up. He turned around and offered a hand down, pulling two other people up behind him.

"Sorry," said the young man, "didn't realise there was anyone else in here." He was wearing a battered old flight jacket and sporting a fairly unimpressive, threadbare moustache he had yet to grow into.

Petru waved a hand dismissively. "It's fine, don't worry, join the party. The old man seems to know everyone else on Netaris," he added, grumpily.

"Oh, we don't know him," said the young man. "We're just hitchhiking into town."

Petru instinctively looked again at the trio. There was a blue-haired girl and another with a scarf over their mouth and straggly, straw-coloured hair who wasn't paying any attention to the conversation. Neither of them dark-skinned, so not their girl.

"Just the three of you?"

"Yeah," said the young man with a smile. "We crashed out in the forest a few days ago. We're trying to get to Gran Palomos to get some parts. I'm a pilot."

"Not a very good one by the sounds of it," grunted Goff. The young man looked uncomfortable, but the blue-haired girl covered her mouth to hide a chuckle.

The truck had started up again by this point and was now bouncing along the roughly-surfaced road. It had been a long time since Petru or any of his men had been in a vehicle that moved along the ground, and they were not enjoying the bumpy ride.

"Surely fliers aren't that expensive," muttered Jekk.

"Quit your moaning," snapped Goff.

Petru watched as the young man and woman exchanged nervous glances. While climbing into a van and finding four armed men sat there would be disconcerting for anyone, Petru wondered for a moment about the three people the student was travelling with. Could they have split up? He reached into his pack for his datapad and pulled up Aecola's record, before leaning forward and holding it out to the pilot.

"We're looking for a student that's gone missing near here, I was wondering if you might have seen her."

The young man took the datapad and looked at the screen. He shrugged, passing it on to the girl. "Like I say, man, crashed a few days ago. We haven't seen anyone, not until this old geezer picked us up." The girl, after a cursory glance, waved it under the nose of their friend before handing it back to Petru.

"Is she in trouble?" asked the girl.

"I hope not. We were called in because her course administrator was worried about her. She was out in the forest doing fieldwork but failed to report in a couple of weeks ago."

The young man made a noncommittal sound and leaned back against the side of the truck. "Well, if we see her, we'll be sure to report it." He bowed his head and within a minute or so was fast asleep.

It was an hour or so later, just as the sun was at its zenith, that the truck took a sharp left, rattled its way across even bumpier ground for a few minutes and then stopped. The old man killed the engine.

In the back, Lukasz woke up from his semi-doze and eyed the soldiers warily. The silver-haired one who appeared to be in charge was stretching. The one with the shaved head was grousing about yet another stop, which in turn was irritating his squad mates.

Turning his head, Lukasz peered out of the back of the truck. "Looks like we're at a farm."

"Of course, it's another bloody farm," grumbled the miserable soldier.

The old man's face appeared over the tailboard, reaching for the pins that held it, and lowered it. He held his hand out to Wiktoria who, bemused, took it and allowed him to help her down.

"Where. Are. We?" said the disgruntled soldier, far louder than was necessary.

"My farm. We stop now, all out."

"Finally," exclaimed the soldier, before turning around and giving his sleeping companion a rough shake. "Tyger! Get up!"

Xin and Lukasz jumped down from the truck, pulling their packs out behind them. "You okay?" asked Lukasz in a low voice.

"Other than shitting myself when he showed us that picture of Aecola?" replied Wiktoria. "Yeah, just peachy."

She turned away and clamped her mouth shut as two of the soldiers helped the third one down. He'd done something to his foot it seemed.

"You need help?" asked the farmer. "Doctor?"

"We'll be fine," said the squad's leader, following his men out of the back of the truck. "You said we're close to Gran Palomos here?"

"Sure, sure," the old man said. He turned and pointed back down the track they'd just driven down, then off to the left. "Two hours, maybe more, maybe less."

"And we can't miss it?"

"The road only goes to Gran Palomos," came another voice, younger, stronger, with the old man's accent but without the same limitation on his vocabulary. "You can't miss it if you just stick to the road." A young man, muscular and stocky, walked over to the truck from one of the outhouses, wiping his hands on a dirty cloth.

"Thank you, you've been a great help," said the senior soldier to the old man. He then turned to the younger farmer. "Before we go, we're looking for a girl, she may be wandering around here lost. Have you seen anyone recently?"

The young farmer shook his head once, then shook it again when the soldier handed him the datapad with Aecola's image on it.

"If you see her, you need to report it to the authorities, yes?"

The young farmer shrugged. "Okay."

The soldier looked at him for a moment, then turned to his men. "Come on, we should get going."

The soldiers started off down the track, two of them still helping their limping companion.

After they had disappeared from sight, Wiktoria crouched down and gently vomited on the ground. Lukasz threw his head back and ran his hand over his face.

"Ohh, brother... Can you believe that...?"

The young farmer gave them a strange look but was distracted by the old man, who was suddenly chattering away at breakneck speed, pointing his arms this way and that.

Xin gestured his head at the old man and flashed his fingers at Lukasz. Lukasz frowned and turned to look at the two farmers. After a moment, the younger one looked up. "You are not friends with the soldiers?"

"No, we are not," replied Lukasz emphatically.

"My grandfather didn't think so. He says you should look in his cab."

Warily, Lukasz walked over to where the two men were stood by the truck. Over their shoulders, he could see into the cab to where a mess of blankets was heaped on the seat next to where the old man had been at the wheel.

Lukasz gave the old man a look, then turned to his grandson. "I don't get it, what am I looking at?"

The old man's face broadened into a huge, toothless grin as he took hold of one corner of the blanket and gently lifted it.

There, lying unconscious on the seat of the truck, scratched and bloody and terribly pale, was Aecola.

XIV

"We really caught a break," said Lukasz.

He walked into the huge low-ceilinged kitchen that was the hub of the farmhouse and took a seat at the long, rough, timber table that ran down the centre of the room. Helping himself to a cup of coffee from the pot, he drained half of it straight off and topped it up again.

Wiktoria and Xin were halfway through a freshly cooked meal of eggs and bacon, accompanied by a local grain hash. As Lukasz was helping himself to the coffee, an old woman, presumably the farmer's wife, brought a plate over to put in front of him. She didn't speak, but smiled a huge, warm smile when he thanked her.

"So how is she?" asked Wiktoria.

"The doctor says the drugs he's given her will contain the infection until they get her to a proper facility in Talos. She should be fine. The infection, left alone, is quite invasive but seems to have little initial resistance to treatment."

"She was lucky he showed up when he did."

"Lucky? Not a bit of it. The old man got him here. He picked Aecola up in a field about ten minutes before he ran into the soldiers. He actually pulled into the doctor's house with them in the back, asked him to follow along behind and come to the farm when he saw the soldiers set off on foot again. Wily old bastard."

"How come he didn't just hand her over when the soldiers said they were looking for her?"

There was a brief pause as Lukasz chewed the forkful of bacon he'd just put in his mouth, then swallowed.

"Didn't trust them. The indigenous population has no reason to love the Netaran authorities, let alone four armed off-worlders who show up looking for a young girl. He knew she needed medical aid, not to be arrested. If everything was above board, it could be sorted out later."

"Is she okay? I mean, is she conscious?"

Lukasz frowned. "She's awake, yeah, but very weak. She's talking about coming with us to Gran Palomos but it's a bad idea. For Litton's sake, we need to press on quickly and she'll just slow us down at this point. Not to mention the need to get the evacuation started. I think it's up to us now."

He didn't even ask if they were willing to take it on. He knew his friends well enough.

The old man took Lukasz's hand in both of his and shook it vigorously, a beaming smile on his face. "We'll take care of your friend. Good care."

"Thank you. We should be back for her tomorrow." He bit back the urge to add, "hopefully."

The old man nodded, still shaking Lukasz's hand. Eventually, Lukasz carefully drew his hand away, giving the old man what he hoped was a reassuring smile. He ignored Wiktoria's smirk.

Lukasz, Wiktoria and Xin were standing in the yard ready to go. They had said their goodbyes to Aecola and were about to set off for the final trek.

"You ready, guys?"

Xin nodded.

"Absolutely," said Wiktoria.

"Hold up!"

Hector, the old man's grandson, emerged from one of the outbuildings, holding his hand up. "I'm heading into Gran Palomos, I can take you."

"Really?"

"Of course, let me just wash up and I'll be right there."

He disappeared into the house, and they waited for a few minutes until he reappeared.

"This is very kind of you, Hector, but if we pass the soldiers on the road, won't they be suspicious that you didn't offer to take them as well?"

Hector gave Lukasz a wide grin, full of teeth.

"My friend, we're not going by road."

Lukasz's teeth were rattling so hard that he was convinced they were about to come loose. Hector's offer, as kind as it was, was one he almost wished they had turned down.

The network of dirt tracks that crisscrossed the farm were, Hector had assured him, a more direct route to Gran Palomos than the road. They would cross the old man's farm in a more or less direct line and meet the road at the far side, undoubtedly ahead of the soldiers. The tracks were far from even, however, and the open-top buggy they were travelling in would have been bouncing them around even at a normal driving speed.

They were not driving at a normal speed.

"Isn't this great?" yelled Hector over the noise of the engine. He turned to look at Lukasz beside him as a particularly sizeable bump in the track lifted the buggy, momentarily, into the air.

Lukasz returned Hector's grin with a markedly fixed one of his own. "Great!" he yelled back.

Hector, still looking at him, took a hand off the wheel to give Lukasz a thumbs up, causing the buggy to lurch violently. The farmer laughed as Lukasz grabbed at the dashboard.

Behind them, Wiktoria was sitting with her eyes closed and her hands gripping the seat as she murmured a prayer to herself over and over.

Xin gazed out over the fields, looking for all the world as if they couldn't be more relaxed.

The going was a lot smoother once they left the farm and got onto the road. As Hector had predicted, they saw no sign of the soldiers. The fact the squad had an injured member meant there was no conceivable way they could have gotten this far yet.

It took about twenty minutes to reach the outskirts of Gran

Palomos. Hector slowed right down as they entered the town, giving the three a chance to get their bearings and form their initial impressions of the settlement.

Most of the buildings were single-storey and the same, uniform beige colour. The roads were still little more than dirt tracks, compacted by extensive use. There were few vehicles in evidence but plenty of people, a fair number of whom waved at Hector as he drove by. They were almost all indigenous, although the odd off-worlder could be spotted among them. At one point, a small gang of children tried to run after them, calling out to Hector until he left them behind in the dust.

The road they followed led them right to the centre of town, opening out into a huge square. Three sides of the square appeared to be made up of bars and shops, the fourth being dominated by a large church, whitewashed and almost glowing in the sunlight.

It was market day. The square was crowded with people. Dozens of roughly built stalls in loose rows displayed mainly fruit and vegetables from the farms around the town, interspersed with the odd stall selling beer or tools and, even more infrequently, more exotic goods, some from off-world. The townsfolk crowded in among the stalls, examining the goods and haggling with the traders, their voices united in one busy chorus. Hector slowed right down as he manoeuvred the buggy through the crowd, occasionally shouting or gesturing at a shopper stoically ignoring them, and eventually pulled up outside a bar. Cutting the engine, he turned to his passengers. "My friend Oolos' place. He has an uplink we can use."

Lukasz, his composure restored by the more placid second half of the journey, clapped Hector on the shoulder. "Thank you, you've been very kind to us."

Hector grinned. "Think nothing of it! Come, let's get you sorted out."

The four jumped down from the buggy, Wiktoria and Lukasz a little gingerly as they made the transition back to solid ground. Only Xin seemed to be unaffected by the off-roading. Lukasz put a hand to the small of his back and groaned a little. Hector laughed and grabbed Lukasz's arm, pulling him into the bar.

The interior was dark, and cooler than the square outside. A handful of men around Hector's age were scattered around but, with the market in full flow, it would be a few more hours until the bar reaped its share of the reward that market day offered.

Behind the bar, a fat man with a sad moustache stood wiping ineffectually at a glass. He was wearing a vest that had seen better days and his hair, what remained, had been cajoled into a fruitless attempt to cover his balding head.

"Oolos!"

The fat man looked up and, putting down the glass and the somewhat unsavoury rag he'd been wiping it with, stepped out from behind the bar to walk over to Hector and give him a warm embrace.

"Hector, you scoundrel! Where have you been hiding, leaving old Oolos here alone?" A few of the customers looked up forlornly, seemingly resentful that their company should be valued so little, before returning their gaze to their drinks.

"Oolos, these are friends of mine. This is Lukasz, Wiktoria and Xin." The barman gave Lukasz an embrace no less warm than he had given his friend, which made Xin step back nervously. Wiktoria was quick to extend a hand when her turn came, which Oolos took and kissed, courteously.

"Any friend of Hector is welcome here. What can I get you?"

"Thank you, Oolos," said Lukasz. "A drink would be most welcome but first, Hector says you have a satellite uplink. We need to borrow it, if we may."

At this, Oolos' face darkened. He turned to Hector and started to speak in the local dialect, quickly and with much gesticulation. Hector cursed.

"What is it?" asked Lukasz, frowning.

Hector turned back to him. "The army came through a few days ago and confiscated Oolos's uplink, along with most of the comms equipment in the town. They had some story about insurgents in the forest being supported by local townsfolk, which is the first I've heard of anything like that."

"It's bullshit, is what it is, my friends," growled Oolos.

Lukasz raised his eyes to the ceiling and shook his head in disbelief. "So, there's no uplink available in Gran Palomos? At all?"

Oolos rubbed at his chins and exchanged a glance with Hector. Hector nodded.

"Well," said Oolos, "There might be one we could use…"

XV

"If he's the mayor, why don't we just tell him what's going on? Surely, he'd just let us use the uplink?"

Oolos spat. "He's a corrupt bastard, in the pocket of the military. The soldiers that took my comms, they were being chauffeured around by his goons. It was him who told them who in town had the equipment. If you go in there and start telling him the military are up to something, he'll hand you over to them before you'll know what's happening."

Lukasz and the others had been shown by Oolos and Hector to a large villa on the edge of town. A well-constructed fence enclosed the grounds, only allowing a restricted view of the beautifully tended gardens and elegant white house within. The five of them were now surreptitiously giving it a onceover from a table on the street, outside a bar opposite the villa's locked gateway.

"You're saying we're going to have to break in?" asked Lukasz.

"I don't like it," muttered Wiktoria.

Oolos shrugged apologetically. "It's the only thing I can suggest. I didn't say it would be easy."

"I don't like it either, Wiktoria," said Lukasz, grimly. "But time's against us. If the only uplink in town is in there, that's where we have to go. Otherwise, we may as well condemn the whole town to infection. We need to alert the proper authorities immediately. There's no time to get to the next town."

As he said that, a figure appeared at the gate, looked up and down the street, before passing out of view again. The man had been armed.

"There's your problem," said Oolos. "The mayor's house is guarded. There's little chance of breaking in without a firefight."

"Great. So, what do you suggest?"

"The mayor's hosting a party this evening and I happen to be very good friends with his cook's wife," said Oolos, with a wink. "They will be getting a lot of food and drink delivered this afternoon, she can get us in."

"And she won't betray us?"

"Betray us? To that bastard?" Oolos spat again. "She hates the mayor almost as much as she hates her husband. She'll relish the chance to put one over on him."

The sun was setting over Gran Palomos as the gate to the mayor's compound was swung open, allowing the truck to rattle in, the unmistakable clinking of many bottles audible from the rear. The driver pulled to a halt at the guard's signal and the two had a brief conversation as the sentry checked his datapad for Oolos' name on his schedule. The guard frowned as he noticed the last-minute amendment.

"What happened to the other guy?"

Oolos shrugged from the driver's seat. "No idea. Had a falling out with the cook or something, probably. Just my luck," he added, irritably.

"You're getting paid, aren't you?"

"Pah! Barely," groused Oolos. "For a rich man, the mayor drives a hard bargain with his suppliers. But I don't want my licence renewal held up, so what can I do?"

The guard fixed Oolos with a hard stare. "You can be grateful for the business, you fat bastard." He lowered his datapad and pointed up the driveway. "Go around to the left of the villa and park next to the other suppliers. And keep a civil tongue in your head."

Oolos put the truck in gear and pulled away, leaning out of the window and gesturing dismissively at the guard as he did so. Beside him in the front seat, hat pulled low to disguise his off-world features, Lukasz was sweating.

"You were taking a bit of a chance there, weren't you? Was that necessary?"

"Forget it, no problem," said Oolos cheerfully. "Everyone hates the mayor. It would have stood out more if I wasn't moaning. Besides, the guard? I've known him since he was a boy, the miserable turd. He is nothing."

Oolos pulled the truck up alongside several others that were parked where the guard had said they would be. A number of townsfolk were milling around, unloading crates and filing in and out through the doors to the kitchen area. Oolos waved at a few he knew as he and Lukasz got out of the cab of his truck.

"So, where's the uplink?"

"Hold on, my friend. I've a truck full of wine and liquor here. I understand your hurry, but I can't keep our cover if you disappear and I have to unload it all myself. They'll wonder why I didn't bring any help." Oolos pointed a chubby finger to the back of the truck where Hector was dismounting. "You get the crates out of there and help set up the bar first."

"But…"

Oolos held up his hands. "I pulled in a big favour to get this job at the last minute, I need to deliver. If you manage to sneak into his comms room and upload your information without being seen, we can all still drive out of here with nobody any the wiser. That won't happen if I mess up this job, though."

"He's right," said Wiktoria, hopping down behind Hector. She had changed out of her blue jumpsuit into a billowy, patterned skirt and a white, low-cut top that Oolos had insisted would make her fit in more. Although she could see other women dressed similarly amongst the various staff milling about, Wiktoria had a suspicion the outfit was more about Oolos's personal preferences than remaining incognito. She'd taken an instant liking to the man, but something about his smile suggested a wicked streak.

Xin dropped down from the truck and started pulling the nearest crate toward the lip of the rear compartment. Very reluctantly, they had taken Oolos' advice as well, tying their sandy hair back and hiding it under a small-brimmed hat, as well as going without their trademark face-covering. Lukasz was still slightly taken aback every time he caught a glimpse of Xin's mouth. Xin would be a ball of nerves because of this, Lukasz knew, and he was impressed at how his friend was handling it.

Wiktoria grabbed a crate and she and Xin headed for the door.

"Come on, we better earn our keep," grinned Hector.

It took the best part of an hour before Oolos was satisfied with how the bar had been set up. By this time, the mayor's wife had appeared and was pushing the staff around, making sure everyone knew exactly who was in charge.

"Our guests will start arriving in half an hour," she snapped, pushing Wiktoria out of the way to rearrange the welcome drinks that Oolos had poured and set out on trays. Wiktoria scowled, until Hector elbowed her sharply in the ribs. Fortunately, the mayor's wife didn't notice and scurried off to berate a young man holding a tray of hors d'oeuvres at a precarious angle.

"We need to find that uplink," whispered Lukasz to Oolos. The bar owner nodded.

"I don't know exactly where it is, but it won't be hard to find. The mayor's office will likely be on the ground floor somewhere. I'd imagine it's in there. If not, the upstairs rooms are your best bet. Luckily, with the guests arriving soon, I expect the household will all be down here in the main reception rooms. Hector and I will mind the bar, I'll get a couple of others to stop what they're doing and help us circulate with the welcome drinks, just until you get back. But hurry. And don't get caught."

"It wasn't my plan to," replied Lukasz, grimly. He fingered the datastick inside his shirt with Aecola's footage on it, to reassure himself it was still there. Then he nodded at Xin and Wiktoria and the three of them slipped out of the kitchen.

The hallway was, for the moment, empty. They could hear preparations and heated instructions being given in the reception rooms to either side, the doors to those spaces being wide open to create one long space the width of the front of the villa. In the hallway itself a grand staircase descended from the upper floor, fanning out to a wide base facing the front doors, its elegant banisters a rich, almost gleaming, dark reddish wood. Tucked behind the other side of the staircase from the kitchen access were a couple of closed doors. Neither were locked. One opened into a small sitting room, empty now. A quick glance around told Lukasz that what they were seeking wasn't in there.

Behind the other door, as Oolos had suggested, they found what was obviously the mayor's office. The three slid into the room as noiselessly as they could and shut the door behind them.

Lukasz looked at Wiktoria and indicated a set of shelves on one wall, then pointed to the far wall and nodded at Xin, before circling around the ornate desk that loomed large in the centre of the room and taking a seat.

Paperwork (actual paper!) was strewn across the desk and Lukasz idly pushed some around until he was satisfied there was no electronic equipment hidden beneath. Opening the drawers one by one to check the contents, in one he found a handgun of an unfamiliar design. In another, he came across a box of local cigars which he helped himself to a couple of, tucking them in his jacket pocket. But there was no uplink.

"Dammit, nothing."

"Me neither," said Wiktoria.

They both looked to Xin, who shook their head.

"Upstairs then."

Lukasz stood up but as he did so, the three of them heard a sound that stopped them in their tracks. Voices, outside the door. Lukasz's eyes flashed a warning and Wiktoria took a swift step to place herself, silently, to the side of the door that would hide her as it opened. Instinctively, Lukasz opened the drawer with the unfamiliar firearm and pulled it out, levelling it at the door.

The handle turned, slowly, then the door itself swung open. The first thing to appear was a man's back, as he backed into the room still facing the woman he was accompanied by. They were kissing, eyes closed as they clumsily pushed into the room.

Wiktoria waited until they were inside and then pushed the

door shut. The click was loud enough to catch the attention of the woman, who opened her eyes even as her lips were still locked on to those of the man. The first thing she saw was Lukasz pointing a gun at her, prompting her to pull away from the man and open her mouth as if to scream. Wiktoria pulled a blade she had secreted in her blouse and quickly held it to the woman's throat.

"I wouldn't."

They recognised the man straight away, Oolos having pointed him out earlier. Shorter than average, with a venomous cast to his face and a luxuriant black moustache, the mayor was well dressed, in a way that spoke of wealth some way beyond what the town had to offer. Interestingly, the woman, who was at least twenty years his junior, was most definitely not his wife.

He looked shrewdly at the intruders, then walked calmly over to his desk. Lukasz covered him every step of the way with the gun he'd retrieved from the desk, taking a step back as the mayor got closer. "I'm warning you…"

The mayor ignored him, reached into the drawer that held the box of cigars and took one out. He paused for a moment as he displayed the cigar to Lukasz, as if to show he had no violent intention, then he put it in his mouth and leaned forward to place the end of the cigar to the barrel of the gun. With the gentlest of touches, he placed his other hand on Lukasz's and depressed Lukasz's finger on the trigger. He puffed a couple of times at the small flame that appeared at the end of the ornamental lighter, then stood back and looked Lukasz straight in the eye.

"You're in my office."

Lukasz, unsure of his next move, continued to point the lighter at the mayor.

The mayor shrugged and sat down in his chair, placing his elbows on the table and steepling his fingers as he turned his attention to Wiktoria.

"If you make any attempt to call for help," said Wiktoria, "I'll slit her throat."

He shrugged again.

"If I call for help and my wife finds me in here with her, she'll do it herself."

The young woman opened her mouth to protest, but the feel of the blade at her throat changed her mind.

Xin, motionless until this point, seemed not to have caught the attention of the diminutive city official. As they stepped forward, the mayor for the first time let a flicker of surprise show on his face. Calmly, Xin pulled their bolt-pistol from their waistband and raised it.

"Okay," said the mayor waspishly, dispensing with the bravado that now seemed misplaced. "What do you want?"

"We're looking for your satellite uplink," said Lukasz, finally putting the lighter down on the desk. "We have an urgent message to get through to the authorities in Talos."

"I'm the authorities in Gran Palomos, give your message to me."

Xin raised the bolt-pistol a notch. The mayor nodded slowly. "Fine. It's upstairs, though, and my guests have begun to arrive."

For the first time, the three off-worlders realised that the gentle hubbub of chatter from outside had taken on a more convivial tone and was louder than when they had crept into the office. Lukasz grimaced.

"That's okay," said Wiktoria. "I'm sure nobody would be surprised by you giving a tour of the house to a few of your guests."

"You're hardly dressed like guests," said the mayor, sardonically.

"Then let's get a move on before more of them arrive," she retorted, giving him her pleasantest smile.

Lukasz stepped to the door and opened it a crack. There were only a handful of people visible in the hallway and, as luck would have it, at that moment the mayor's wife appeared and ushered them through to one of the reception rooms. Lukasz turned back to the room.

"Let's go."

Luck was with them. They made it to the upper landing without being seen and the mayor gestured down a hallway. Passing about a dozen doors, he finally halted not far from the end of the corridor.

"I'm reaching for my keys," he said as he put his hand in his pocket. Xin, standing back in order not to be caught by any sudden movement, watched him carefully but the mayor seemed to have no desire to complicate the situation. He did indeed retrieve a set of keys from his pocket, identify one and use it to open the door. With a sarcastic flourish, he gestured to the group to enter. Lukasz went first, followed by Wiktoria, still holding her knife to the young woman's throat. The mayor raised his eyebrows at Xin, who indicated with the barrel of their bolt-pistol that the mayor should go first. They slipped in behind the hostages, pulling the door shut behind them.

The room was another office although, unlike the one downstairs, clearly not intended for receiving guests. The desk, still an elegant piece of furniture, was smaller, more functional. There were bookshelves again, but less in the way of ornaments. There were no pictures on the wall. There was a very definite sense that this was the mayor's private retreat; there wasn't even a second chair in evidence.

On the desk there sat a monitor and, attached to it, the uplink. Lukasz hurried around to the other side of the desk and powered up the computer. The desk unit hummed as it sprang to life. Lukasz, after a brief pause to familiarise himself with the interface, accessed the required portal. He took the datastick from inside his shirt, inserted it into the unit and began the upload, using the secure address connected to the University of Talos that Aecola had briefed him on.

He slumped back in the chair, watching the screen. After a few seconds, an anticlimactic ping confirmed the data had been sent.

"And we're done," muttered Lukasz.

XVI

And yet, not quite. Lukasz pulled a handful of security ties from his pocket that Oolos had given him, just in case, and secured the mayor and his companion to the legs of the heavy desk. "I've no doubt it won't be long before you're found, they're probably already looking for you, but we just need enough time to slip out of the kitchens. If the data we've sent has the desired effect, the planetary authorities should be descending on Gran Palomos within the hour, but to be honest, I don't want to hang around and undergo a lot of questioning." Once the ties were secure, he pulled a couple of cloths from his pocket and gagged them. "If we slip away now, I'm sure they'll be too busy to start looking for us. I don't think we'll meet again. Cheerio then and thanks for the use of your uplink."

The mayor shot him a disdainful look from behind his gag.

Lukasz looked up at Xin and Wiktoria. "Let's go."

Xin opened the door a crack and peeped out into the hallway, checking the corridor and towards the stairway. After a moment, they nodded at Lukasz and pushed the door further, stepping out into the hallway. Wiktoria and Lukasz followed.

"Hold it!"

The voice came from behind them, from the tail-end of the corridor they'd assumed empty.

Before they could turn to see who had spoken, two men appeared ahead of them in doorways near the stairs, one on each side of the hallway. Neither stepped fully into the open, just made themselves visible enough to show they were armed.

They were surrounded.

"Turn around, slowly."

Behind them stood two of the soldiers from the old man's truck. The silver-haired squad leader had his pulse rifle raised and pointed straight at Lukasz. Next to him, the disgruntled soldier with the shaved head had one hand holding a bolt-pistol firmly to the temple of the young, sick-looking woman whose arm he held in his other.

Aecola.

Lukasz felt sick. They must have thought something was up, doubled back and searched the farmhouse after he and the others had left. Maybe they saw the doctor arrive.

"The data this woman gave you," said Petru, in no mood for preamble. "Give it to me."

"What data?" replied Lukasz, innocently, hoping his face hadn't given anything away when he'd seen Aecola. Maybe they could bluff their way out of this yet...

"He said hand it over!" Jekk swung his gun around to point it at Lukasz. His voice cracking, he trained the gun back on Aecola. "If you don't hand it over right now, I will shoot her."

"Woah, woah..." Lukasz held his hands out low. "Calm down. We..."

"*Hand it over!*" Jekk was sweating now; and he started to back away towards the end of the corridor.

"Jekk," said Petru quietly. "Leave this to me..."

"No, Captain, you've had your chance, I'm *done* with this. This mission has been a catastrophe from the start!" Jekk's hand holding the bolt-pistol was trembling now and he swung it between pointing at Petru and Lukasz, before once again putting it to the side of Aecola's head. "You've ballsed this up, Captain. Tyger's wounded, Zane's *dead*. For all we know, we've all been exposed to that *shit*. Now they're going to hand over the data *right now* or I'm going to kill her."

Wiktoria spoke up. "The data's gone. We've already sent it to the university. It's over."

Jekk let out a low, desolate moan. His face white now, he rubbed at his head with the butt of his pistol, then used his sleeve to wipe the sweat from his eyes.

"Stand down, Jekk." Petru took a step towards him but froze when Jekk turned the pistol on him.

"Stay still, dammit!"

"Okay, look, you want it? Take it," Lukasz reached slowly into his pocket and pulled out the datastick and held it out towards Jekk.

Jekk ignored him, his attention now on Wiktoria. "You sent it?"

She nodded. "It's gone. It's been uploaded. Whatever happens now, it'll be decided away from here. By others. Our part in this, all of us, it's over now."

Jekk let out another chilling, inhuman moan. "It's all been a waste…"

Petru gave Wiktoria a questioning look, to which she gave an almost imperceptible nod in response. His shoulders dropped. He had no idea who this woman was, but he somehow knew she wasn't lying. What else would they have been doing in that room? The mission was over.

"Jekk, we're finished here. Missions fail. It happens. We're done now." Petru took another step closer.

"*No!*" The crackling hum of a bolt-pistol sounded and Petru dropped to the floor, clutching his shoulder.

Behind them, Lukasz could almost feel the other two soldiers' uncertainty paralysing them. One of them called out to Jekk but he ignored them.

"I've trekked for days through that bastard forest to stop this bitch and now you're telling me I'm too *late?*" His voice reached a crescendo as he pointed his weapon at Wiktoria.

While his attention was focused elsewhere, Lukasz tried to make eye contact with Aecola, but she was clearly still too sick from her infection to register what was happening. He cursed inwardly.

"Look, Jekk? I know…" started Wiktoria, in a placatory tone.

"You know *nothing!*" Jekk let out one more final howl of frustration and turned the gun back on Aecola.

Once more, a bolt-pistol hummed.

XVII

Petru concluded his report and stood silently, still at attention.

"And can you explain to me, Captain, just *why* you shot your fellow soldier to protect this fugitive?"

"The mission was over, Colonel. At this point the data had already been sent. There was nothing to be gained from killing the civilian."

Petru's superior eyed him from beneath his formidable, wiry eyebrows. The debrief was taking place in a tent on the outskirts of the forest, where the first stage of the infection control operation was being mounted. Outside, scores of soldiers were suiting up and checking their flamethrowing equipment, ready to embark on the scorched-earth treatment that would, unfortunately, be required to clear the Eschatonus infestation from the affected area. Safe to say, none of the men outside were privy to the nature of the discussion occurring within the tent.

"She was a fugitive, a criminal." The colonel was pacing up and down, trying to keep his temper in check.

"Not in any official sense, sir."

"But she knew what had happened, how the Eschatonus arrived here. And you saved her by killing one of your own men?"

"Perhaps we should just let the captain explain his own actions, Colonel Slem."

The interruption came from a third man, the only other occupant of the tent. Not visibly military, the rather anonymous man was dressed in an unremarkable suit and was perched on an uncomfortable-looking stool at a small folding table. In front of him was a thin dossier containing just two sheets of paper. He was, at that moment, polishing his glasses.

Petru continued. "The civilian's status as a fugitive was not official, as the operation was black, sir."

"Don't talk to me like I'm an idiot, Petru, I know all this."

"It was my assessment, in the moment, that killing her would verify her story in the public's eyes, not quash it. Indeed, silencing it was no longer an option, the data already having been sent. If she had been killed, people would want to know why. However, given that she walked away and can now freely return to her studies, the only possible conclusion will be that the military has no issue with her or her actions, thus verifying what I assume will be the official story. That the activity she recorded was that of a rogue element within the military acting without orders."

The colonel grunted. "That's as maybe, but you still shot one of your own men."

"Jekk was out of control, sir. He was no longer responding to my orders and was about to kill the girl. Morally, I felt that this was unjustified and unfortunately the only way of stopping him shooting her was to shoot him."

"What the hell has morality to do with it?"

"Furthermore, he had also just shot his superior officer." Petru's arm was bound and still numb from the treatment he'd been given for the wound. "The mission was over," he repeated. "It was a failure, but either way, it was over. As of that moment, the situation involved a dangerous, out-of-control soldier threatening the life of an innocent, officially, civilian. That alone was enough to justify my actions. The fact that it also lends support to the official account of what's transpired here is additional to my defence."

The colonel stopped pacing and grunted to himself. Drawing himself up to his full height, he continued, "You did fail, Captain. You lost men, including one you killed yourself, and you failed in your mission. Without the loss of the population at Gran Palomos, the government is unlikely to secure the required public support for the latest round of deregulation. And the financial cost of this clean-up operation, not to mention the loss of life, will all have been for nothing. You realise that you'll be the one who's held accountable for all this."

"I do, sir." Petru's face didn't even flicker as he replied.

"I'm not so sure," said the third man, replacing his glasses and folding the small cloth he'd been using, putting it away in his jacket pocket.

The colonel turned on him, eyes blazing. The man ignored him and calmly closed the dossier on the table.

"Captain Petru, it seems to me quite clear that in the official account of this episode, you will be exonerated. Your part in the Eschatonus infestation being the result of a deception from a superior officer, you acted in good faith, believing the mission to be legitimate. Furthermore, when you started to have doubts about said legitimacy, you were then instrumental in both saving the life of the young woman and in the timely notification of the planetary authorities that saved the population of Gran Palomos..."

"This is outrageous!"

"In fact," continued the man, "I wouldn't be surprised if there was a promotion in your near future, Colonel Petru."

"You've no authority!" barked Slem.

"I'm afraid it's your authority that's to be questioned, Colonel Slem, given you were the superior officer who ordered the mission."

Slem's face blanched. "But... but I've been loyal..."

The third man for the first time looked the colonel in the eye. "Some men instinctively understand what's required in these matters, Colonel. They are able to analyse facts, interpret changing circumstances and make decisive judgements in the moment. These are the sort of men that are useful to us. These are the sort of men that we can trust, rely on. Other men do not have those skills and so are less useful to us. Colonel Petru? You'll see to Colonel Slem's detention, pending trial for treason and conspiracy."

Petru looked at Slem, the old man's face crumbling as tears formed in his eyes. This was all making Petru distinctly uncomfortable. "I..."

"It wasn't a suggestion, Colonel Petru."

The flier swooped in over the canopy and landed next to the *Farewell to Tethree*, the long scar in the forest caused by her emergency landing a more than adequate landmark with which to find her. Lukasz and two medics jumped down almost before it stopped and quickly unloaded a medi-pod. The medics followed Lukasz to the ship's cargo ramp. Opening it, he indicated with a gesture the direction in which they needed to go.

A few minutes later, they reappeared, the medi-pod floating between them. Lukasz breathed a sigh of relief as he peered into the pod and made eye contact with a pale but conscious Litton. Lukasz held up a hand, not sure if the sedated student would even register him, but Litton returned the gesture, so far as he was able to move his good arm within the confines of the pod. After all that had happened, the fact that they had got back in time to save the young student made Lukasz more emotional than he had anticipated. It was the one final piece of the mess that had needed sorting and Lukasz felt a great weight finally lift from his shoulders.

Wiktoria and Xin, unloading a small number of containers bearing the ship components they had been given, likewise stopped to check the pod as it passed. Xin reached out and put a hand on the pod, Wiktoria putting her own hand on Xin's shoulder. They watched the pod being loaded onto the flier then continued to unload the gifts they had received from the grateful citizens of Gran Palomos, along with a few crates of wine from Oolos.

A thin and unsteady Aecola climbed down from the flier and made her way gingerly over to Lukasz.

"You didn't have to come all the way out here," he said, as he held out an arm to steady her. He guided her over to the ramp where she was able to sit.

"I'm fine, just a little tired is all. I wanted to see you off. See you all off," she corrected herself, averting her gaze briefly. "I didn't get the impression you were going to hang around."

"I think the townsfolk of Gran Palomos would have been happy for us to stay as long as we wanted," grinned Lukasz. "But no, Colonel Petru was tactful but very clear. The planetary authorities are grateful for our assistance in dealing with this threat. However, our arrival on the planet was never officially cleared, due to the circumstances under which we arrived, and therefore it's been decided that our swift departure would be easier for everyone concerned. Less paperwork. And before anyone starts asking awkward questions about unauthorised off-world interference in a domestic Netaran situation."

Aecola shivered, "That sounds like a veiled threat."

"I don't think he intended it to be veiled."

Aecola shook her head. "It's outrageous."

Lukasz shrugged. "It's fine by me. I'll take a swift good-bye over a prison sentence, any day." He regretted the way it sounded the moment he said it. He looked down at the young woman. Something about the way she looked, even recovering from a potentially deadly infection, made his heart race a little faster. He wanted to reach down and comfort her but didn't.

"I had hoped you'd stick around. For a little while, I mean." Aecola looked up at Lukasz, not entirely managing to disguise the hope in her voice. He was once again struck by the beauty of her violet eyes.

For a moment, neither of them said anything.

Wiktoria broke the silence, passing them as she carried the first of the containers up the ramp. "Lukasz, move yourself. Xin and I aren't loading all of this ourselves." Aecola looked away to the flier as Lukasz turned to face his engineer.

"What happened to 'Captain'?"

Wiktoria paused on the ramp, giving Lukasz a disdainful look.

"When we're flying, then you're the captain."

Lukasz muttered something under his breath and started off towards the flier.

Wiktoria looked down at Aecola, who looked back up at her.

"I'm sorry," said the engineer.

"I know," sighed the student. She pushed herself up from the ramp and made her way back carefully to the flier.

Wiktoria watched her go. The girl's feelings were as transparent as they would be fleeting, no matter how all-encompassing they felt right now. Confusing gratitude with a genuine emotional connection was easily done, but Wiktoria knew Lukasz. He wasn't going to be hanging around. Delaying the inevitable wouldn't do Aecola any favours.

Wiktoria adjusted her grip on the container she was holding and carried on into the ship.

END

ABOUT THE AUTHOR

Ray Adams

An avid reader of sci-fi and fantasy since his early years, Ray Adams has yearned to be a writer since childhood. A passion for political and philosophical debate, as well as the arts in all its forms, and a strong personal interest in mental health issues, shapes the worlds he is bringing to life in his sci-fi.

The Roo Raka Trilogy, the third and final part of which was published in 2021, is his first series.

He writes under the big skies of Norfolk, England.

BOOKS BY THIS AUTHOR

The Forcek Assignment

A quiet life on the fringes of society is all Roo Raka wants. Regular work, enough to keep his crew happy, and if it strays into grey areas of legality then, well, a little bending of the law never hurt anyone. Not anyone who didn't deserve it, at least.

There's always a bigger picture to consider though, and after he runs into trouble on what should have been a routine cargo pick-up, Roo Raka finds himself drawn into a web of conspiracy, a plot that's aimed at the heart of Galactic government. As those in power tighten their grip, and law enforcement cracks down on an increasingly unhappy populace, plans are drawn up and there's a decision to be made. Can Roo Raka stand by and ignore everything he sees around him? Is it really nothing to do with him? Or does there come a time when a good man no longer has the luxury of doing nothing?

The Jollet Procedure

After the events of The Forcek Assignment, Poonsar is left devastated by the fate of his captain, Roo Raka, and retreats to his homeworld under a dark cloud of depression. Bo Dans and the rest of the crew of the Lady Julian meanwhile go in search of a new strategy to combat the Memm. Does the answer lie outside the Federation with a rogue scientist? How will they extract this scientist from the clutches of the Committee? And will Poonsar be able to fight through his mental anguish and rejoin them in their mission?

The Last Sanctuary

Roo Raka's body lies dead, his consciousness downloaded into a hard drive through a revolutionary and dangerous procedure. Though with no way of reuniting his body and his mind, and the Galactic government set on retrieving the mysterious entity known as the Memm, the crew of the Lady Julian are fast running out of options.

With the clock ticking, an unlikely connection offers them sanctuary but with the net tightening, their safety is far from guaranteed. And just as it feels as if there's nowhere left to run, something stirs in the darkness...

Playtime's Over

(as James Kinsley)

In the seconds before death, Will finds himself transported from the depths of the North Sea to the end of a deserted pier. Deserted, until Viktor appears... Together they journey across time and place, bearing witness to the beauty of the life Will has turned his back on. scrutinizing the interminable balancing act of being alive, which ultimately led Will to make his final, fatal move. Playtime's Over is a story about resilience and surrender, told with darkly absurd humour. It is both a powerful meditation on mental health in a world with little refuge, and a touching portrait of a friendship forged in the most bizarre circumstances.

Printed in Great Britain
by Amazon